Charles Maurice Davies

'Verts, or, the Three Creeds

A Novel: Vol. II.

Charles Maurice Davies

'Verts, or, the Three Creeds
A Novel: Vol. II.

ISBN/EAN: 9783337067113

Printed in Europe, USA, Canada, Australia, Japan

Cover: Foto ©Andreas Hilbeck / pixelio.de

More available books at **www.hansebooks.com**

THREE CREEDS.

A Novel.

BY

Dr. MAURICE DAVIES,

AUTHOR OF "UNORTHODOX LONDON," "BROAD CHURCH," ETC.

" The Bee and Spider, by a diverse power,
Suck honey and poison from the selfsame flower."

IN THREE VOLUMES.

VOL. II.

LONDON:

TINSLEY BROTHERS, 8, CATHERINE STREET, STRAND.

1876.

LONDON:

SAVILL, EDWARDS AND CO., PRINTERS, CHANDOS STREET,
COVENT GARDEN.

CONTENTS

OF

THE SECOND VOLUME.

BOOK II.—ALEC LUND'S LETTERS.

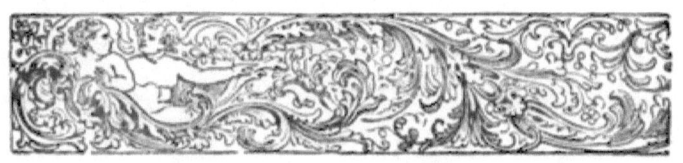

'VERTS.

BOOK II.—ALEC LUND'S LETTERS.

CHAPTER I.

THE STATUS QUO AT ZOAR.

DEAREST ELSIE,—I arrived here soon after Briggs's telegram was sent off; and as that, I have no doubt, has alarmed you, I will not lose a post in communicating; but I have so much to tell you, that although this will very probably be expanded into a voluminous letter, it is still possible my information may fail to be exhaustive. Indeed, I feel that I can scarcely grasp the condition of things myself, much less convey it to you.

"In the first place, be assured there

is no cause for alarm, nothing which calls for your immediate presence, though I should not wonder if this letter winds up with a postscript asking you to get leave of absence from Mrs. Fane and join us here for a few days. Women always shy at a telegram, and jump to the conclusion that somebody is dreadfully ill. Nobody is ill in body, though I cannot say the state of things is at all what I could wish in Zoar.

"Let me follow your example, and write my letter in a measure diary-wise, taking up the journal of events, in fact, where you broke off. I promise, however, to abstain from those mysterious asterisks which you affected in the concluding pages of your annals.

"When I arrived at Zoar, I went straight to Briggs's lodging, as I thought I should hear more from him about the true state of affairs than from anybody else. Of course he thought I had come in consequence of his telegram, in which case I must have travelled by telegraph myself. When I told him I had simply looked in, so to say by accident, he was struck with the coincidence. He congratulated me on my success in the matter of the fellowship, and evidently thought me a maniac for not holding it awhile when I had got it. True to the spirit of your asterisks I did not tell him the reason—not then.

"Briggs does not know any of your people, as you are aware; nor is he very accurately posted up in the gossip of Zoar. As long as he keeps clear of cold, and sings a true G at service, then his object in existence seems to be attained. He knew, however, some little about my anxiety as to certain of your belongings, and was alarmed to see this morning the house and business in High Street advertised for sale. Rumours of ugly proceedings in reference to your father were rife, and he thought you or I— you see he brackets us as far as that particular conjunction can do it—ought to be on the spot. We have reason to thank him for his promptitude.

1—2

"From Briggs's lodgings in the Vicar's Close, I sped at once to High Street, which was, surely enough, shut up and placarded with notices from garret to basement that the house and furniture were to be sold under a bill of sale, and the old and valuable business disposed of.

"I noticed as I went down the Vicar's Close, that Mr. Moddle was at his window and 'spotted' me. Directly I had passed, he was out and off like a shot in a different direction from that in which I was going. I knew what that meant; he was going to apprise Percy of my presence in Zoar. When, therefore, I knocked at the side door in High Street, I was not at all surprised to see Moddle and Percy posting along as fast as their legs would carry them. I got in before them, however, and found your father and mother alone. They looked harassed and dejected, and I thought seemed rather to resent my intrusion. I knew we should not have time for a long story before Percy and Moddle were upon us, so I solved the mystery of the asterisks in your diary at one bold stroke; that is, I took our marriage certificate from my pocket, laid it on the table before your father, and said—

"'My dear sir, I can see you ask for an explanation of my apparent intrusion. There it is. Not a soul knows of our marriage as yet. Elsie would not allow herself even to write it in her diary until you were made aware of it. Will you forgive us?'

"'Married! thank God!' was what your father said. Your mother's exclamation was 'pure womanly.'

"'Dear Elsie, is she well?'

"Before I had time to answer her by more than a look, Percy and Moddle burst rudely into the room. Had I been as well aware of your father's feeling towards me—towards us—as I am now, I think they would have left even more abruptly than they had entered; but we had no time, as I tell you, to exchange a word on the subject.

"Your father and mother seemed quite scared, and evidently feared a commotion.

You know I can command my temper, and Percy proved the same fact on a certain memorable occasion which you have not forgotten, neither had he. I therefore resolved to prevent any outbreak by being excruciatingly polite, yet taking the bull firmly by the horns. It is always the best plan.

" ' How do you do, Mr. Percy Llewellyn ?' I said—to which, by the way, Mr. Percy Llewellyn replied never a word. ' I have had the pleasure of meeting you before, but your friend has the advantage of me in that respect. You are surprised, no doubt, to see me in Zoar, perhaps still more so that I venture to break in upon Mr. William Llewellyn's privacy at such a moment.'

" ' Not at all surprised,' Percy said, with the faintest suspicion of being severe ; and old Moddle echoed him in a very hollow reverberation—

" ' Not at all surprised.'

" ' My authority for presenting myself is that I am now a member of the family'—I tossed the marriage lines to him as I said this—'and, as Elsie's husband, my place is, of course, here.'

"'Married!' said Percy, with a slight change of countenance; 'the ceremony followed closely upon my Aunt Phillis's death, sir.'

"Poor fellow; it was his last Parthian shot. I smiled, and said in my blandest tone—

"'Yes; Miss Llewellyn's death removed the only slight obstacle there was to our union.'

"'One obstacle,' suggested Percy; 'but there may be others.'

"'Too late, my dear sir, now, as that document will show you. I have another,' I added, 'which I copied at Doctors' Commons, and about which I shall have to ask some information at your hands. As the matter is purely legal, it will be best transacted at your office, where I will call upon you to-morrow morning if you will allow me. If you have business with your uncle now, I will leave you and call upon the Dean. I have scarcely had time to introduce myself to my father and mother-in-law yet; but as I know this is a critical period in their fortunes, I would not for the world interrupt anything you may have to say.'

"Moddle, I could see, was inclined to stop; but the mere mention of Doctors' Commons acted like a spell upon Percy. He immediately discovered he had an appointment elsewhere, and the two left together. 'Arcades ambo!' was my mental ejaculation as I bowed them out. I found myself doing the honours of High Street at a moment's notice. I wish you had been there, you would have enjoyed it.

"Well, then I came back and sat down with your father and mother. We had a long chat, and I venture to think they approve of their son-in-law. I told them that our united incomes, though not very large, were quite sufficient even at present to enable us to offer them a home; but as yet they do not seem able to realize the fact that the old home will avail them no longer. Your father is for the moment crushed by the blow which has fallen upon him ; and which I have not the slightest doubt has been intentionally brought about by your Uncle Edward, acting in the background through Percy and Moddle as catspaws. I hazard a further conjecture that Sam is the mainspring of all the mischief. The event—for I mean that there shall be an event—will show us whether I am right or not.

"At first your father and mother would scarcely listen to me when I hinted at this. I knew I must approach the matter cautiously ; but I really was not prepared for their obstinate incredulity. Your father is so good and frank himself that he cannot fancy anybody else being different. Edward has done his best to 'pull him through' his difficulties, he thinks ; but he says he was gone past redemption. The leech was applied too late. He cannot see that this leech has been sucking at his system for years. Your mother is positively awe-stricken at your aunt's genteel deafness and

Sam's venerable beard. If an archangel had told her that Edward and Sam were anything but immaculate when first I opened fire, she would have repudiated the suggestion. I don't think they are so much biassed in favour of Percy; but Moddle has a great hold upon your father as being an 'Angel' in the chapel, where I find your parent is only an 'Evangelist.'

"In order to get anything like a hearing then, I had to detail my visit to Doctors' Commons, which I am reminded is a secret even from you. You only know vaguely that I got a trump card on that occasion. I have been holding it back so far; now I mean to play it—soon, that is.

"'Impelled by what I had heard from Elsie'. (for you must now suppose me to be addressing your parents), 'I journeyed all alone to Doctors' Commons determined to devote a day of my not very valuable time to discovering the archives of the Llewellyn family in the shape of their testamentary arrangements.

" ' First of all, I set myself to explore the last will and testament of Morris Llewellyn (that is your grandfather, you know. These parentheses are yours, Elsie). There I found that the business in High Street was left to William Llewellyn, as a set-off against certain moneys which had been advanced some years ago to article Edward, and to set up Sam in his mysterious and still undefined business. There was an annuity to be purchased for his sister Rachel. His daughter Phillis was to be residuary legatee of his personal estate, and the Topaz Farm was to be equally divided between the four children.'

" ' Just as I told you,' said my father-in-law.

" ' Exactly what Edward always said to us,' added his wife, as if she were really glad to find that the family respectability was intact, though that very circumstance involved her own ruin.

" ' The will,' I continued, ' was drawn by Llewellyn and Son—that is, I presume,

Edward and Percy—and attested by two of their clerks, so that they could give you all information so far.'

" ' Oh, it's as clear as the day,' said your father, relapsing into his former moody condition, which I did not at all like to see, ' there is no hope to be derived from the Topaz Farm. It was left between us all, and Edward has simply bought up our shares. To be sure mine was valued very low, and an idea did strike me that the valuer had been tampered with by Edward.'

" ' What nonsense,' said your mother.

" ' Yes; I think I was unjust to Edward,' remarked your father, in a tone which it made me almost angry to hear.

" ' Allow me to continue,' I rejoined. ' It is quite impossible that such clear-headed lawyers as Llewellyn and Son could have drafted that will without looking back one stage to see whether Morris Llewellyn had the right thus to dispose of the property— unless there was some reason for suppressing any question in the matter. Do you follow me ?'

" They both said they did ; but I believe they were romancing. They thought I was going to draw on my imagination, my prejudice, or what not ; but I soon interested them when I came to facts.

" ' At all events,' I proceeded, ' I looked that one step further back, whether Llewellyn and Son did or not. I ferreted out the last will and testament of Mistress Susanna Dash——'

" ' And there you found——'

" ' Yes. Now I am going to astonish you. I am going to tell you, not what I think or hope, but what I have seen and know, and what, if I may be allowed to say so, it seems rather extraordinary you two have not taken the opportunity of learning long ago.'

" ' What is it ?'

" ' Simply that you, my dear sir (I was addressing your father, Elsie), were the real heir of Mrs. Susanna Dash. Your father had an interest in the Topaz Farm only until you should come of age, when it became yours absolutely.'

"'Mine?'

"'Yes; the will seemed loosely drawn enough. Was there, may I ask, any doubt whether you would reach maturity?'

"'I was a delicate child, and it was supposed I could not be reared. It was that, I fancy, which gave Mrs. Dash her interest in me.'

"'So I gathered from the wording of the will, which was evidently designed so as to let the farm revert to your father supposing anything happened to you.'

"'Edward can have had no idea of the contents of Mrs. Dash's will,' said your father, 'or—to put it on your own footing, to take no higher ground—he would never have risked his position so far as to ignore it in the one he drew for my father.'

"'Never,' echoed your mother. 'He is so respectable.'

"'Now you must pardon me if I differ

from you both on this point. It is, I say, simply impossible that they could have failed to look back that single step.'

"'But how do you account for the risk being incurred?'

"'It was a bold stroke, and no doubt they counted the cost. Besides, my very dear father and mother (we will leave out all allusion to the law in *those* titles, at all events), you are so exceedingly easy in these matters, and credit Mr. Edward Llewellyn beforehand with so much respectability and goodness, that I am very much afraid he traded on this.'

"Your mother looked daggers at me, Elsie. Your father sat holding his head, as though he were determined to keep con- viction out of his brain as long as possible.

"'Then,' I continued, 'what is more to the point still, Elsie, as she often says to us, made the mistake of being born a woman instead of a man. She was engaged betimes to Mr. Percy Llewellyn, so that no one could ever have any interest in raising in-

quiry as to the inheritance. It was I who
unwittingly crossed the calculations of these
good gentlemen.'

"I am sure your mother at that moment
wished, as devoutly as Edward himself, that
I had never stepped in to interfere with
family arrangements.

"'That two lawyers so far-sighted as
Edward and Percy Llewellyn should not
calculate contingencies was,' I went on to
say, 'impossible; but it was quite possible
that father and son should each leave out of
the category of such contingencies the probability of the latter being jilted by Elsie,
or cut out, as the phrase goes, by so very
unlikely a personage as myself or anybody
else, for the matter of that. When family
or personal pride comes in to blind the
judgment, even long-headed lawyers err occasionally.'

"Your father's grip on his poor forehead
was a little relaxed, which I looked at as a
symptom that he was coming round; but
your mother had got ready a clincher for me.

" 'You see, Alec'—I was glad to hear
her call me by my Christian name, though
it was evidently with an effort—' supposing
matters were as you I am sure honestly
believe them to be, the transaction could
not have been carried through without
Uncle Sam's knowledge and connivance;
and he really is too good and religious for
me to believe such a thing possible of
him——'

" 'And poor Phillis,' your father cut in,
laying ruthless hands upon his cranium
once more, ' she had a cold sense of duty
enough, but I am sure she would never
have lent herself to fraud.'

" 'That I am quite willing to believe;
and, trust me, my dear parents, it is only
with the most extreme reluctance I thus
act the part of iconoclast, and pull down
the venerable statues in the family Pan-
theon. Of the dead we would speak nought
but what is good, and I can quite believe
that Miss Phillis Llewellyn, if she were
privy to this scheme at all, agreed to it

under protest. What could a woman do? I myself believe that the knowledge of the scheme accounts for her constant aversion from Percy's ministrations. Elsie was always puzzled by this; I suspected the reason years ago, but now I know it. I *must* speak thus positively because the existence of the plot is as clear to me as my own existence. I have seen it in black and white in that cold-blooded will at Doctors' Commons, and,' I added, with as much sternness as I could assume, 'I really do not think you ought, either of you, to shut your eyes to your own and Elsie's interests —my interests, if you like—simply for the sake of bolstering up a previous belief in people who do not deserve your confidence——'

" 'But, Sam——' your mother was going on: I interrupted her.

" 'Sam, if I may forbear to garnish his name with prefix and suffix, has been very accurately described to me by Elsie, and I know him to be eminently religious—to be even now on an evangelizing tour in the north of Ireland.'

"'Sam has been here for weeks, helping to pull me through,' your father said; "actually neglecting his own business in London to come and settle mine.'

"'What!' I exclaimed. 'Sam been here for weeks? Then that Irish tour was a blind.'

"'What do you mean?' asked your father; and even your mother looked inquisitive.

"I told them the history of Sam's nocturnal exodus on his alleged tour of evangelization; and they seemed a bit staggered by it—principally, I think, because the information came from you, not from me. Clearly, they have not quite got over the impression common to so large a portion of the Zoar community, that I am a 'dangerous man.'

"'Sam evaporated mysteriously during the night after T. and P., as I told you, giving it out that he was off for Ireland.

2—2

Elsie said she knew Patty was fibbing at the time.'

"'Poor Patty,' your mother said. 'Surely you don't think *she* belongs to the conspirators?'

"A very beautiful trait, Elsie, is that obstinate conviction that everybody is honest and good, and that whatever is, is best; but sadly unpractical in this work-a-day world, and this age of stucco and veneer. It's safer, though not so amiable, to adopt the maxim of Edward and Percy, and believe everybody is taking you in, and that words are meant to conceal thoughts.

"I have taken up my abode in High Street, and am finishing off this just as you used to post up your diary—after everybody else is gone to roost. I have managed during the evening to extract from your father the following information, all of which confirms to the utmost my previous conclusion.

"Directly after you left Zoar, the enemy,

who had been working covertly beforehand, made open advances. I wonder whether they suspected you or me, that they were so anxious to get you off the ground first? Perhaps they realized the force of that graphic adage that the power of two is so much more than twice the power of one. At all events it is quite evident they were afraid of you, and determined to bring matters to a climax, since you had gone over to the enemy. The long and short of it is, Edward, who had got your father into a hobble by persistently demanding the very exorbitant interest which he exacted for his accommodations, suddenly discovered that he must have the principal repaid too. By a strange coincidence Sam simultaneously made the same discovery. The Topaz Farm share failed to supply material for so large a haul; and the determination was come to that the business must be sold. Even that might not realize enough; so the house was to follow suit. ' Really, William, you will be more comfortable in a cottage in

the suburbs of London,' said Edward.
'Somewhere near me, and dear Patty,'
blandly suggested Sam; and the thing was
done, and the house and business advertised
before your father knew where he was; your
two rejected suitors, Percy and Moddle,
surveying the proceedings with a Mephistophelian grin.

" Between ourselves, dear Elsie, I think
the old folks will be better off in town with
us, but as far off as possible locally and so-
cially from Sam and Patty. The business
is not what it was. Things have moved on
since your grandfather's days, and your
parents are, in one expressive word, too respectable to keep pace with the progress of
modern trade; let us say, not to give
offence, too static, too conservative of old
traditions. Let the house and business go.
This will have the effect at the same time
of allowing your eminently respectable
uncles and cousins to take rope enough
Edward says there will be a nice little sur
plus to form a nest-egg for the old people's

future support. I don't believe there will be a fraction; but Edward and Sam—when they have had their quantum of hemp—shall disgorge every penny, or my name's not Alec Lund.

"How strange it is to picture our changed conditions! Here am I in your sanctum, where you used to write all those treasonable letters to me, while Percy was the nominal lord of your affections; and you are in London, reversing the order of things by working, whilst I am comparatively idle. Not that I plead guilty to being really so. I am working out that which shall 'to all our nights and days to come, give solely sovereign sway and masterdom,' as Lady Macbeth says. But I am sadly forgetting my poor newspapers. I wonder if they would like a series?

" 'Papers from Zoar!' It would puzzle even a special correspondent to find material for a graphic letter here, I think.

"It strikes me that if we really carry out our project of preserving this strange family history for our possible offspring and those whom it may concern, your diary, now concluded, would form, as it were, the first volume, and these letters the second. What the third volume will be remains uncertain ; but I feel that the hidden fires are becoming active within the volcano. Just you amuse yourself with editing these letters, then. I shall write daily, of course, and you can suppress any portions that do not seem relevant to the story, linking the rest together in any way that seems to give coherence and continuity to the narrative. I would, I think, omit all dates, and just run it on with a few dashes of your own pen where such may be necessary to make the story a consecutive one.

"Having taken up my abode at High Street, I made it my business, on the morrow of my last letter, to call upon the Very Reverend the Dean, your former friend and fellow-student. As I was going to the Deanery, I met your quondam rival too, Mary Baker. I ventured on a little quiet 'chaff' as to Cousin Percy, telling her you were disposed of now, and there was no reason why he should not make her his wife. I think Mary is prettier than ever, and I felt quite alarmed at the effect my words produced upon her. She first turned crimson, and then became so deadly pale that I thought she was going to faint.

"'Why, Mary,' I said, 'what is the matter? You don't mind my joking you, do you? You know we unintentionally acted eavesdroppers at the stile by the Fishponds once; but I didn't mean to hurt your feelings.'

"'No, it was not that, Mr. Lund; I know you are my friend,' she replied, 'but—but——'

"'But what, Mary?'

"'I wish you could make your words come true.'

"'What! you've lost your heart to the parson, have you? I thought it was only a mild flirtation?'

"'Oh no, I *do* love him!'

" ‘Do you indeed, now?’ I said. ‘Well, there is no accounting for tastes. Miss Llewellyn, you see, had the bad taste to prefer me. But may I act Father Confessor so far as to ask whether Mr. Percy Llewellyn loves you, too?’

" ‘Yes—no—that is——’

" ‘Ah, I see. He is having a flirtation with you, and you have gone farther than he, and fallen in love?’

" ‘How did you know that? You read me like a book. Have you been eaves-dropping at the Fishponds again?’

" ‘What! you make that still your trysting-place, do you? Well, Mary, yours is not a very uncommon case, I fear. No, I have not been listening; I only guessed.’

" ‘Is it so common?’

" ‘Well, I rather think yes. Does he know you love him?’

" ‘Oh yes.’

" ‘Does he ever speak about marriage?’

" ‘Never.’

" 'Will you let me give you two pieces of advice, Mary?'

" 'Certainly. I am sure you would only advise me for the best. What are they?'

" 'In the first place, be on your guard against Mr. Percy Llewellyn. He may do you a mischief.'

" 'No, he loves me too well for that.'

" 'Of course you think so. Take my advice, nevertheless.'

" 'Well,' she replied, looking amazingly pretty and coquettish, and as though she would be perfectly ready to have a flirtation with me on the spot, married man though I am, 'and what is your second piece of advice, Mr. Father Confessor?'

" 'Tell your mother all.'

" 'All I have told you?'

" 'Everything; whether you have told me all or not.'

" 'I cannot,' she replied, blushing crimson again.

" 'Why?'

" '*It would kill her.*'

"I drew my own inferences more from the girl's manner than her words, though they were emphatic enough. There was nothing in what she had told me calculated to kill her mother, though enough to alarm her. One is apt to say 'Am I my sister's keeper?' in a case like this; but I think I shall give Mrs. Baker a word of advice when I call upon Aunt Rachel, as I shall be in duty bound to do. And yet I have so much on my hands at the present moment in reference to Mr. Percy Llewellyn, that this love-affair with the pretty milliner would complicate matters terribly. When the girl left me I promised to meet her at the same place the day after to-morrow (I hope you wont be jealous), and I hoped to hear either that she had extracted a promise of marriage from his Reverence, or that she had confessed her indiscretion to her mother. It is rather cruel to Mary, I fear, but I have an idea I should like to make Percy marry her.

"The Mary Baker episode over, I sped to

the Deanery, and found the Very Reverend couple all anxiety to hear about you. Mrs. Dean bantered me a good deal upon having cut out the Calvinistic cousin and then leaving my wife to work like a Hottentot Venus whilst I went competing for fellow-ships I did not want and had no right to get, and then recommenced loafing about Zoar as of old, while my wife slaved away in the ignominious position of a daily governess.

" ' And pray how did you know I had a wife?' I inquired. ' I hoped to have had the pleasure of conveying that information to you.'

" ' Did you not mention it confidentially to Briggs ?' responded Mrs. Dean. ' And what has that poor little precentor got to do between services, if not to run about the streets of Zoar and circulate such pleasant news ? I am convinced he could not have sung the service if he had not confided in the Dean first.'

" ' And how is Mrs. Lund?' said the Dean ; ' and what—what are you doing ?'

"I told him of your exceptional post as governess to Mrs. Fane, and of my great success in the journalistic groove, at each of which he shook his Very Reverend head in quite a Jupiter Olympius style.

"'You don't congratulate us on our start in life, sir?'

"'Both very well for stopgaps and to bolster up a—will you excuse me?—somewhat imprudent marriage; but each too precarious to bring up a family upon.'

"Then I told him we were going to start with a family ready-made, by having your father and mother to live with us; and I was astonished to find how much he knew of the ins and outs of your father's affairs. Of course Briggs is responsible for that too; but I thought the Dean's interest in the Llewellyn family stopped short at you.

"'Ah, a bad business, I'm afraid,' were the words he slowly enunciated when he had done shaking his head. 'A very, very bad business. That Bishop's secretary will overleap himself if he does not take care.'

"'I believe he has overleaped himself already. I hope so.'

"'Take care what you are doing,' the Dean replied, in his most mysterious tone. 'Your new relative is one of the most unscrupulous of lawyers ; and they are very dangerous animals—very dangerous animals, indeed.'

"'But there are others still more so.'

"'You allude to Sam Llewellyn in particular——'

"'And money-lenders in general.'

"'Yes,' the Dean replied ; and heaved a great sigh, as though he too had known what sixty per cent. meant calidâ juventâ.

"'I am now going to beard the lions in their den,' I said, still more surprised to hear that the Dean knew my relatives even by name. He could not have had dealings with Sam. It would have involved an anachronism to think so. 'I am going to bring these good people to book.'

"'Have you counted the cost of the warfare ?'

" 'I have;' but it occurred to me I had not.

" 'And do you think you are equal to a brace of unscrupulous lawyers—I call Percy Llewellyn a lawyer rather than a Gospeller—with the probable addition of that very astute Nonconformist, Moddle?'

" My mind misgave me that the odds were rather long on the opposite side. But what was I to do?

" 'I should insist upon seeing one at a time—beating the enemy in detail, even if so you would beat them—or, if they declined that, I should claim the right to have a witness or witnesses present at the conference, man for man.'

" 'But I hardly know whom I should select as my champion. My father-in-law——'

" 'Would be the very last person in the world. He would ruin all.'

" 'I really know nobody else.'

" 'There is Briggs.'

" 'For a mute personage, he might do.'

" ' You really want nothing more. If a third person is required I will be present myself.'

" ' How can I thank you ?'

" ' Don't thank me at all ; because it is purely on your wife's account, not yours, that I consent to mix myself up in a very disagreeable family quarrel—for such I fear it promises to become.'

" Isn't that Dean a very reverend brick, Elsie ? I had no more idea of his taking up the cudgels for us, than of Jupiter himself coming redivivus from the Capitol, or any other of his quondam abodes, to guide the course of terrestrial justice into a right channel. I am exercised to think what a bombshell in the enemy's camp this brace of dignitaries will be, but especially the Dean. If we could only substitute the Bishop for Briggs, the effect would be indeed terrific. I am scribbling these reflections in the Dean's study while he arrays himself for the attack. He has sent for Briggs to join us. I will resume when the conference closes.

"We sallied forth from the Deanery after a precociously early luncheon, the Dean deeming it wise to fortify the material man against any demands that might be made upon it.

" 'Never sign yourself impransus if you can help it,' he said, 'on the eve of any great undertaking. How the great lexicographer ever got through his magnum opus under such conditions I never could understand.'

" Briggs and I let the Dean have all the talk ; not so much from modesty on our parts, for I think Briggs is properly conscious of his own merits, and you know I am, do you not, Elsie? But I rather think the little precentor felt somewhat nervous as to the result of the encounter. As for me, the mere walking up and down the streets of Zoar in company with the Dean and an inferior dignitary was a new sensation. As the simple townsfolk doffed their hats, and clearly included me in their comprehensive salute, I began to realize a new sensation—something of the monstrari digito order—and to wonder whether I should ever sally forth in those reverend habiliments an object of awe to admiring parishioners. I believe you sometimes picture such a sólution of the problem, Elsie, if one could look quite down into that little heart of yours. I feel very much inclined to write something spoony here, and to necessitate more asterisks in event of publication. But I will refrain.

"The record would be imperfect, however, if I did not take into account the quietude and tranquillity which seemed to pervade the tiny city. I thought of you amid the roar of London—thought of the horrible lawyers boxed like some voracious animals in their kennel of an office, awaiting our arrival; and as the autumn leaves fell from the lindens on the cathedral green, I half came round to your way of thinking, and wondered why we could not be content to

3—2

let things rest. Life is before us, and we are in a fair way of success. Why not leave the lawyers to their paltry triumph? I did not awake from my brown study until we got to your uncle's office; and then the sight of the brass plate with 'Llewellyn and Son' on it, dissipated all my peaceful ideas at once. I was as eager for the fray as the carnivorous gentlemen within.

" 'Mr. Briggs and I will sun ourselves outside awhile. It is a favourite walk of mine, and he is a frequent companion in my peregrinations. My advice to you, Lund, is to hear much and say little. You hold, as you tell us, a trump card. Don't play it rashly. Although held in a lawyer's office, this is really a family council. As such, if you like to call in your friends, you can; but I have no doubt the family element will soon give place to a forensic one. Then we must retire; and you will confide your interests to a professional man.'

" 'To Sheppard, of course.'

" 'To anybody you like. I fancy it will

be another drop of bitterness in the cup of woe, will it not, if Edward Llewellyn has to come into contact with Sheppard. He considers himself a cut above him.'

" ' As the heavens above the earth.'

" ' Poor fellow !'

" The clerks in Edward Llewellyn's office, as is the custom of their kind, assumed the most complete stolidity when I entered and asked whether Mr. Edward, or Mr. Percy Llewellyn, could be seen. First they looked despairingly at one another, as though the request were per se monstrous. Then they hazarded a conjecture that both were engaged ; and finally they did what I knew they were going to do, ushered me into where a triumvirate was seated, violently doing nothing at a table in your Uncle Edward's private office. The trium-viri were Edward and Percy Llewellyn, and —Mr. Moddle.

" At the farther end of this not very extensive apartment was a door ajar. It might have led to a cupboard, or safe, or another room; but, whatever it was, I felt morally certain Sam was inside, just as poor old Hugh Latimer heard the scratching of the pen within the fireplace, that was covered up on the occasion of one of his numerous compulsory visits to the Bishop of London. *He* was the Dangerous Man in his days. Heterodoxy varies like the modes of *Le Follet*.

" Percy and Moddle greeted me as—well, as one man who has been cut out by another generally does greet his successful rival; but your Uncle Edward went in for the affable rôle, at all events as a commencement. I wondered whether he had seen me in company with the Dean and the precentor on the other side of the way; but I think he had not.

" After the usual overture on the subject of the weather, and tender inquiries as to the probable duration of my stay in Zoar, Edward opened fire. Looking vigorously for nothing amongst his papers (that is a way lawyers have), he said, as if by way of afterthought—

" ' You are come, no doubt, to consult us in reference to poor Phillis's will.'

" ' Not at all. That is out of your hands I know,' was my answer. A good raking shot at the beginning shows you mean business, so I continued, ' I shall consult Mr. Sheppard on that subject, as he has, I find, drawn up a later will than that made by yourself and your son.'

" Mr. Edward Llewellyn—for I ought not to speak of him irreverently as Edward—reddened all over his Charles James Fox face, and said coarsely—

" ' Then, if that's the case, what the deuce have you come here for ?'

" I smiled, as I fancy I can smile, somewhat sardonically, at his warmth, and said—

" ' That matter is out of your hands ; but I have been searching the wills of Mr. Morris Llewellyn and Mrs. Susanna Dash at Doctors' Commons——'

" ' The deuce you have !' rejoined Edward, indulging once more in his favourite expletive, and getting slightly apoplectic in his visage, ' and what is that to me, pray ?'

" 'Something to you, perhaps; but a very great deal to my father-in-law Mr. William Llewellyn.'

" ' How so ?'

" 'The Topaz Farm was left to Morris Llewellyn only for his lifetime, and then reverted to William Llewellyn, lapsing to a stranger if William died before his father.'

" 'I am glad you are saying this before witnesses. It's an infernal slander! Take it down Percy; listen, Moddle;' so Percy wrote, and Moddle listened as desired, while the mysterious door at the end whobbled backwards and forwards as though it had the palsy.

" ' You have two witnesses here, I know, in fact three, for your Evangelical money-lending brother is behind that door'—this at a venture—' but I have my witnesses too.' I had risen as I spoke, and made a faint sign to my two dignitaries, who crossed the road and walked into the inner office without ceremony, followed by the awe-stricken clerks.

" 'Outsiders *are* to be summoned into the family conclave, Mr. Dean,' I said, 'so I make no apology for asking you, out of the interest you take in my wife, to be present at this interview. Mr. Briggs will stand over against Mr. Moddle, and Uncle Sam is hors de combat,' I added, for the door at the end shut with a bang when the brace of clerics came in. Perhaps Sam thought T. and P. were imminent.

" 'Indeed, Mr. Lund, but I must apologize to Mr. Edward Llewellyn for this intrusion, which, as you rightly say, is made solely in the interests of my most excellent and esteemed friend, your wife. Will you allow me to be present as her representative ?'

" Edward Llewellyn was in a fix. Here was the realization of his wildest dreams possible. He and his deaf wife might dine at the Deanery—possibly at the Palace itself —if he were only a little concessive. The introduction would come as it were through me—that is, through us, Elsie—which

would be unsatisfactory; but the end would
excuse the means. I seemed to have caught
your mantle on my shoulders, and to have
the power of seeing what was passing in
your uncle's mind. But on the other side
of the table Percy scowled, and Mr.
Moddle sneered. The Evangelical had a
soul above dignitaries, and the Nonconformist scorned all 'cloth' but his own.
How was Edward to propitiate the Dean
and save his dignity? He solved the
problem with lawyer-like dexterity.

"'I need scarcely say,' he observed, in his
most unctuous manner, 'that I should be
proud and happy—both my son and myself
would be proud and happy to have the
valued assistance of the Dean of Zoar in any
family colloquy, especially since he honours
one member of that family by condescending
to represent her very humble interests.'

"I never felt so much inclined to kick
any man, Elsie, as I did your venerable
uncle at that moment.

"'But,' he continued, 'this has, I regret

to say, ceased to be a family colloquy. Mr. Lund has imported an element into the discussion which at once assumes a grave legal aspect and touches the honour of our family and firm very nearly indeed. That being the case, I cannot, as you will see, Mr. Dean, consent to enter upon it in this desultory and informal manner. You will pardon me, I am sure. My son, I think I may say, coincides with the view I take.'

" ' Quite,' growled Percy, feeling himself appealed to ; and as for Mr. Moddle, he had got his hat on ready to depart and by way of showing his disrespect for dignitaries.

" A fatuous smile played over your uncle's somewhat expansive visage as he accompanied the two parsons and myself to the door. The Dean, alas ! did not ask him to call, and the prospect of passing the magic portals seems, I fancy, a little farther off than ever for your esteemed relative.

" As to our own affairs, I think the Dean felt he had done a good day's work. He had shown himself effusively polite as far

as you and I were concerned, yet avoided
coming into collision with the lawyers. He
and Briggs, indeed, had acted as a sort of
soft ecclesiastical buffer, and mitigated the
force of the crush between me and your
relatives. It must come, of course; but I
think, with your very reverend friend, that
it had better come in a court of law and
under proper professional guidance than
irregularly at a semi-legal, semi-domestic
conclave in the back-office of one of the
litigants.

"'Go to Mr. Sheppard at once, Lund,'
said the Dean. 'The other matter is in his
hands—I mean the will business. Consult
him as to your Doctors' Commons discovery
too, and leave yourself in his or in other
competent legal hands. You know I am a
little sceptical as to the researches of you
amateur lawyers. Good morning,' he added,
as we came to the door of the Deanery.
'Will you and Mr. Briggs come to dine
to-day?'

"I excused myself on the grounds that I

wanted to concert measures with your father ; and Briggs begged off in the capacity of my quasi-host, responsible for my entertainment at such times as I was not occupied in family affairs.

" ' Unsociable fellows ! Adieu.'

" I am not at all sure that I have handled my trump card adroitly; indeed I feel a disagreeable conviction beginning to steal over me that I have prematurely shown my hand to the enemy. Supposing matters to be as I understand them—and the Doctors' Commons documents appear to me to be so plain that he who runs may read them— that trump card would have formed a splendid dénouement in case of the lawyers pushing matters to extremities. Now I fear I have warned them. They see me here on the spot and are pretty well convinced that my presence means mischief. Here I shall stay, however, until they have done their worst. I am preparing material for a series of articles on the Agricultural Labourers' question, which will at once utilize my residence here, and prevent the newspaper authorities from illustrating in my case the old proverb 'Out of sight out of mind.'

" When the evening lamps were lighted to-night, and your father and mother and myself were cosy around the fire—for we have begun fires already and your maternal parent lets me smoke my cigar—I had a very characteristic conversation on the position of affairs, which goes far to convince me we had better let things take their course here. Give these lawyers rope enough and hope for the happy result. Your mother is as incredulous as the Dean as to my reading of the Doctors' Commons instruments. Anybody would imagine that, because I was born before the days of School Boards, therefore I cannot read the English language.

" ' Depend upon it, Alec,' she said, ' either you have made a mistake in reading these wills, or grandfather Llewellyn and Mrs. Dash made some mistake in drawing them up.'

"'Anybody has made a mistake, my most irritatingly good-natured mother-in-law, rather than Llewellyn and Son—is it not so?'

"'I don't think they would run the risk,' she replied.

"'That is the strongest argument for your view of the case; but then the two interests were to be united by Elsie marrying Percy, so that in all human probability the question would never be raised. They were quite certain neither of you would ever raise it. Lawyers trade on this knowledge, you know.'

"Hereupon your father struck out quite a new line.

"'After all,' he said, 'what does it matter?'

"'What does it matter!' I re-echoed. 'Would you like to make Llewellyn and Son, Solicitors, a present of your worldly possessions? They haven't left you much to give away; but will you placidly let all go?'

" ' Quite. The dispensation will soon close in, and what will it matter who has the trumpery estates then ?'

" ' But in the meantime one must live, and you are not exactly a chameleon so that you can exist on air. You don't mean to die just yet, my very good father-in-the-law, do you ?'

" ' I don't mean to die at all,' he answered.

" ' Indeed. What, have Mrs. Girling and her Shaker friends given you the recipe for immortality ?'

" ' Mrs. Girling hasn't; but Mr. Moddle has. The members of the true church will not die but will be caught up alive into the air at the Second Coming, which is immi-nent.'

" ' And this is Mr. Moddle's theology, is it ?'

" ' It is the doctrine of the Catholic Apostolic Church, to which I rejoice to say I was introduced by Mr. Moddle.'

" ' And you are not in the least shaken by Moddle's desire to marry Elsie and secure the Topaz estate himself ?'

" ' On the contrary, Moddle was the only man who knew how embarrassed I was and how hopelessly all my interest in Topaz had gone. His desire to marry Elsie could have had no mercenary element in it at all events.'

" I do not think your mother, Elsie, believes quite so implicitly in the Catholic Apostolic ' angel' as your father does ; but she preserved an auspicious silence, and I felt it was useless, and perhaps unkind, to say a word against your father's firm persuasion.

" After all, I asked myself, when I came to reflect calmly on this matter, grotesque as this faith appears to me, is it not, in the case under consideration, doing exactly what a religious faith ought to do, keeping its possessor calm and unmoved in the midst of trials under which many a man would break down? Your father's equanimity is not, as I had fancied, mere apathy, but proceeds from the real conviction that the ' dispensation' is closing in ;

that the good time so long coming is all
but come, and that Topaz estates will not
be lacking in the city with the Gates of
Pearl. I ask myself again and again, as
we have often asked ourselves together,
dear wife, is not such an attitude of mind
to be envied? I own I do not like the
Moddle element in the matter. I dis-
believe in Moddle myself; but then that
may be because he was a rival candidate
for your hand. I think it is the firm faith
I have in you that makes me want to feel
faith 'all round' as the saying goes. Your
father urges, reasonably enough, that every
system must have its human instruments
and agents; that the church is militant
here in earth, and must often fight the
world with the world's own weapons. He
wants me particularly to attend the service
at the Catholic Apostolic Church, and if I
can conquer my repugnance to Moddle, I
mean to go. I wish you were here that we
might study it together.

"Clearly I must act Cerberus here until

the lawyers have done their worst. I know
my enemies now, as the Dean said. I have
to face the two lawyers in the open field,
with Moddle as a possible reserve force, and
money-lending Sam sneaking in the background. I wonder whether it would be
possible to win Moddle over to our side.
Shall I pretend to be 'verted; or will
you come to Zoar, and tempt the angel to
a Platonic flirtation? He could be made
a very useful ally, and may prove a trouble-
some enemy.

"What a happy family you would all
be, if I had never joined it and brought
the apple of discord. You and Percy would
have been married and mansioned at Topaz;
your father and mother, having been immo-
lated on the altar of your uncle's dignity,
would have been left to your tender mercies,
with considerable prospects of a shabby-
genteel existence for the rest of their days;
and when the Augean stable of the High
Street shop had been quite cleared away,
Edward Llewellyn and his deaf partner

might have sat below the salt at decanal and episcopal boards. All this I can see was in train; when lo, the evil genius Alec Lund, the Dangerous Man, comes upon the carpet and leads you from the paths of rectitude. In a moment all is changed; and as for my Mephistophelian self, I seem destined like the historic old man and a certain noble animal to please nobody while displeasing myself by my absence from my darling wife. You can burn the rest of this letter if you want to end a chapter, or pepper it with some of your favourite asterisks if you don't.

" P.S.—I warned you as to the probability of such an appendix—if you can without inconveniencing Mrs. Fane get leave of absence for a few days and run down here, I think your presence would be advantageous, and I am sure it would be a comfort to the old people. Give 'that big lad's' compliments to your cruel taskmistress, and ask whether she will remove her iron grip from your neck for a brief space.

CHAPTER II.

WHAT MEN CALL GALLANTRY.

DEAR MRS. FANE,—You are certainly the promptest person I ever knew. When I appended that postscript to my letter, I did not mean that my wife should so literally take the wings of the morning and set off post haste to join me. Let me thank you, however, for your ready acquiescence with our wishes. Elsie arrived quite safely; she joins me in my acknowledgments of your kindness; and, no doubt, this letter, though commenced by me, will be the joint production of us twain.

"It was quite advisable that Elsie should come. The dear old folks simply sent her out of the way of annoyance; but they want her. They are just like two grown-up children, and the big brother has bullied them dreadfully. Of course my presence has stopped all personal annoyance, but I want to be off and stump Arcadia, with the view of writing a series of letters on the agricultural question, and Elsie will be an excellent substitute, for they all stand more in awe of her than of me. The two discarded lovers sank into their very boots directly they found she was on the spot.

"Now let me post you up in all the news from the seat of war.

"In the first place I have consulted Sheppard, the second-rate lawyer here (second in position but, as compared with Edward Llewellyn in talent, Hyperion to a satyr), who counselled patience and a defensive attitude. Let Edward take possession of Topaz, or let him sell the house and business in High Street, and then we are to open fire. He has done neither one nor the other. No notice to quit has been received by the tenant at Topaz. The rents have been received as usual by Edward Llewellyn, who always acted as collector for the family. It remains to be seen what he will do with them.

"Directly after I had posted my last letter, and in consequence, no doubt, of my presence here and visit to the office, reverse notices were posted over the announcements of sale in High Street, stating, in rubricated letters like one of your ritualistic missals, that the sale was postponed. So our counter-move has done something, if only in the way of throwing obstacles in the enemy's advance.

"Before Elsie arrived I complied with my father-in-law's request, and attended the Irvingite service which is held in a large tumbledown building once occupied as a provincial theatre. It was a curious phenomenon on the whole, showing what freaks the religious imagination will play when once let loose. The main portion of the service, which only lasted an hour altogether, was taken by Moddle, gor-

geously arrayed in some vestment designed,
I should think, by himself, and executed no
doubt by a local milliner.   Mr. William
Llewellyn, who is an 'Evangelist,' preached
for about ten minutes, very lucidly and to
the purpose; and then one Daniel Wall, an
inspired cobbler, who is called a 'Prophet,'
uttered a rodomontade from the middle of
the congregation.   It was largely composed
of interjections, and destitute of any coherence; part of it was even in mere
gibberish.   That was called an 'Unknown
Tongue;' and the whole utterance was
regarded as a spiritual revelation.   My
poor father-in-law booked it all religiously,
I could see, in the blank pages of his bible.
As we were walking home together he
asked me what I thought of the service.

" ' Very impressive on the whole.   Almost Roman in ornamentation of ritual.
What would Edward Irving have thought
of it?'

" ' We have developed since his time.'

" ' You have indeed.   Not a symptom of

frigid Presbyterianism in your elaborate cultus!'

" ' But the prophecy.'

" ' That I cannot appreciate. To me it seemed worse than ridiculous—profane.'

" ' So, no doubt, did many utterances of Ezekiel or the herdsman of Tekoa?'

" ' Yes; they were all one with the revelations of the Pythoness. I quite acquit the speaker of conscious imposture ; but I do not believe it was a revelation of the Divine Spirit.'

" ' It was either that or mania.'

" ' An awkward alternative, but very likely a true one.'

" We did not recur to this topic. Can you guess the reason why ? I think so.

" Since I have known you intimately, and especially since my marriage with dear Elsie, I have, as you may have seen, altered my attitude in religious matters. I once gloried in unbelief myself, and longed only to convert Elsie to my way of thinking. Now I *want to believe ;* and I bitterly repent having (as I fear I have) shaken Elsie's mind from the old moorings. I hope and think that my mental constitution is logical. Therefore, I go on to argue that, as there is not a fixed definite standard of right and wrong in these matters, I have no business to disturb the faith of any other person. That person may be right, and I may be ruinously wrong. That inspired cobbler seemed grotesque—or worse than grotesque —to me; but so, no doubt, would Ezekiel or Amos, as my father-in-law most pertinently suggested. That was the first idea which crossed the minds of the 'authorities' in reference to the Apostles; they were mad or worse. We are apt to think everybody so hopelessly insane if they differ one iota from our own preconceived ideas. I can imagine two possible panaceas for such rampant bigotry as, in my better moments, I protest against: one is the philosophic toleration of all forms of faith or non-faith, which I believe never has been fully realized, and perhaps is not feasible; the other is the practical panacea of an Infallible Church. Has that ever been realized, I wonder? Have men, since the very earliest days of the infant Church, been of one heart and one mind? What a glorious ideal it is! I know that you, like myself, pant for the cessation of this Babel-strife about indifferent things.

" You will excuse a theological essay, I know; for, down beneath the surface, you and I are greatly at one on these matters, and so is dear Elsie too. There must be some common ground on which we could all take our united stand and then agree to differ. I often think I discern such neutral territory in the doctrines of the immortality of the soul, and conscious existence after so-called death. That seems more than ever a standpoint now that my own affections have been strongly called forth, and I feel that I could scarcely wish for survival, nay, should almost choose, if choice were allowed, a destiny of annihilation, unless Elsie and I were sure to be together in the next stage of existence. And yet there are some, I fancy, who would tell me that I am making too much of human affection; that I am putting it in the place of the Love of God, when I say this. It seems to me that if my nature were to be so changed by death that I ceased to love Elsie supremely, that *would* be annihilation. It would not be I who should survive, but an utterly different person.

"This is really the aftermath of a long conversation Elsie and I had to-day, when we had been wandering over some of the old haunts we used to frequent in those heretical days before we were man and wife together.

"'How wonderful; how almost impossible it seems, Alec, does it not?' she said, 'that you and I can have a *right* to be walking thus, hand-in-hand, among the Zoar woods and meadows!'

"'Stolen sweets are said to be the most luscious of all. Does not the circumstance of Grundy being propitiated destroy the glamour?'

"'Not for me; and, Alec, I do not think it does for you.'

"'So lately silvered with the beams of the honeymoon, I must be fickle indeed if the glory thus soon departed.'

"'Now, accepting the probability of immediate and continuous existence after so-called death, with the additional advantage of renewed association one with the other, do you not think we shall fall as readily into the new régime there, as we have here?'

"'Quite as naturally, and gracefully, dear Elsie; for I have no doubt we do look more at our ease, and therefore more graceful than when you used to be always peering over your shoulder in dread of spies, and forced me to take giant strides to keep pace with those rather protracted extremities of yours, as you fled panic-stricken from some familiar form in the distance.'

"Elsie, I may mention, has turned in and is sleeping unromantically, not without symptoms of an impending snore, or I daresay this passage would be cancelled. Those legs are rather a sore subject with her.

"'I do not,' I continued, 'believe in that word supernatural. Whatever change supervenes upon us will come, depend upon it, just as naturally, just as imperceptibly as this change in our relations to the Zoar fields and streets. Very likely we shall stalk, as what Longfellow calls "quiet, inoffensive ghosts," about the old familiar places, and wonder why people are not frightened at us, just as we now wonder why the Zoar Grundies have ceased to molest us since those few words were monotoned to us or about us, by that mild curate at St. Cyprian's.'

"It is into this desultory discussion all by myself I have been led by that visit to the little Irvingite chapel—I beg its pardon —to the Catholic Apostolic Church of Zoar. The cathedral is innocent of any appellation half so portentous.

"One man clings tenaciously to a revived

apostolate, another to a magical change
in the sacramental elements *ex opere
operato*, yet another to the correct cut of a
vestment, and graceful pose in a genu-
flexion. Why should they not? If they
derive edification or comfort from these
matters, then, relatively to themselves,
these matters are of vital import. To me
the one absorbing question of all religion is
simply what Keats called 'the grandeur of
the dooms we have imagined for the mighty
dead.' That seems to me the preliminary
fundamental question of all; but, bless me,
one day I may change too, and build ex-
clusively on birettas and auricular confession. Let us above all things be philo-
sophical. Why should not my father-in-
law credit his inspired cobbler? Who am I
to say him nay?

"Since last I wrote, I have had my
interview with pretty little Mary Baker,
which I told Elsie was coming off, and I
know she read you my letter. You must

be thoroughly posted up in all the gossip of Zoar, and the archives of our family: I have a family now; I have passed out of my Melchizedek condition, and am the centre of a family circle, as it is very evident to me every man was meant to be. No truer words were ever penned than those which record the great principle, 'It is not good for man to be alone.'

"As it was important on all accounts that I should keep my interview with Mary Baker private, I was considerably annoyed to recollect that she had named as our rendezvous that very field by the Fishponds where Elsie and I had of old been unwilling witnesses of the interesting tête-à-tête between Percy and Mary. I particularly did not wish to embroil myself with Percy in this matter, having quite scores enough to settle with him already; and I was conscious that there was no place where I was so likely to be 'caught' by him as just there, where lay his road to St. Simon Magus. Elsie and I had got so used to calculating the chances of detection in former days, that we knew exactly the advantages and disadvantages of every field and lane within a radius of several miles. I was half inclined to send Elsie in my place, only I felt that would be mean, as it would be certain to bring disagreeables upon her if Percy found her speaking to Mary, though he could not suspect her of love-making, as perhaps he might do if I were the delinquent. However, I would, as our old habit was, trust to luck, though I wished the little puss had chosen any other spot on the habitable globe rather than this one.

"We very nearly had our first matrimonial quarrel as I was setting out. Up to this time we might have gone in for the Dunmow flitch; and really this is such a trifle, that I am ashamed to write about it; but I suppose the earliest tiff between man and wife always marks a kind of epoch.

"'Elsie,' I said, snappishly enough, for I was irritated with the business I had in hand, 'it's getting quite dark, and I don't want to have the credit of acting the Lothario to a pretty milliner in the Zoar lanes; you might help me to get off.'

"'Your humble servant to command, I am sure,' said Elsie, who was most perversely reading the paper, and, I fear, did not improve my previously indifferent temper. 'What does the lord and master require?'

"'Don't chaff, Elsie.'

"'I never chaff, Alec; I am most serious.' Of course I knew she wasn't. 'What can I do for you?' she continued, with the utmost gravity.

"'Simply find my other glove. I've only one, and I can't go out so this cold autumn night, I shall be frozen.'

"'By all means let us obviate such a catastrophe;' and she sought diligently, but could not find it. This little grievance, added to the former great one, had the effect of putting me in a thoroughly bad temper.

" 'I have a great mind,' I said, 'to give up this matter altogether. You don't seem to care about it; why should I?'

" 'Don't talk nonsense, Alec,' said Elsie, laughing, 'you are put out. You know you don't really mean to sacrifice this poor child because you have lost a glove.'

" 'Don't you put things in a ridiculous light. It isn't only the glove——'

" 'No, the place of rendezvous annoys you, I know, and it is unfortunate; but make the best of it.'

" 'All very fine,' I replied, pulling my hat over my brows, and going forth like a martyr, with my single glove. 'And you know I have to be off the very first thing in the morning, to do those confounded bucolic papers. How shall I get on without my glove then?'

" 'You choose to go by the parliamentary train. You could go by the next without being ruined, and I venture to say you shall have a pair of gloves, if Zoar can supply them, ready for your journey. You can have them now, if you will wait ten minutes. No? Well, it would make you late, I suppose; kiss me and be off. Don't *pout*, as you used to say to me.'

" So I kissed Elsie, felt rather better for my little escape of steam, and set off towards the Fishponds, among the bats and owls.

" I have a habit of reasoning with myself as I go along, and took myself pretty severely to task for the little passage-at-arms I had just had with Elsie. Addressing my sole remaining glove—a dirty, worthless dogskin affair—in much the same way as Macbeth did his imaginary dagger, I said—

" ' You mean-looking brute! It was scarcely worth while to let such a scurvy thing make mischief between man and wife.' And as I was passing the moat round the Bishop's palace, I felt very much inclined to throw the offending article of attire into the water; but on second thoughts I changed my mind, and said—

"'No; I will keep this glove, and its fellow when I find it, not so much by way of memento as to our first quarrel—which I should be glad to forget—but as a reminder not to let my temper get the upper hand of me. I know how soon a home is made wretched by such petty bickerings. It is the little rift within the lute——'

"I was timing my footsteps along the lane to the rhythm of Tennyson's most musical lines, and when I came to the memorable stile, there was Mary waiting for me. The grey mists were creeping up the meadows, and long shadows from the opposite wood lay black across the footway. The girl looked prodigiously pretty, and I could not rid myself of the idea that if anybody saw me, they would sadly misinterpret my motive for meeting her in that clandestine way.

"'I was almost afraid you had forgotten me, dear Mr. Lund,' she exclaimed, putting her arm quite confidentially through mine, for all the world as Elsie used to do, and as, no doubt, Mary was in the habit of doing with her clerical swain. I felt quite easy, because Elsie knew of our meeting, and I cared for no one else.

"'A silly accident delayed me.'

"'An accident!'

"'Scarcely worth the name. I lost my glove first, and then lost my temper with my wife in searching for it.'

"'Naughty man.'

"'And now I have come, what are you going to tell me beyond what you said the other day?'

"'Nothing. I said too much then.'

"'Either too much or not enough. I tell you what I should like you to do, Mary.'

"'What?'

"'See my wife.'

"'Your wife? What for?'

"'Tell her what you won't tell me. Shall I ask Mrs. Lund to meet you?'

"I am very much afraid Mary said, 'Bother Mrs. Lund!'

" 'No ; if you won't talk to me,' she went on, pouting most prettily, 'then I shall just keep my troubles to myself.   I have no one else to talk to, and I did think you were my friend.'

" 'There is Percy——'

" 'Percy I told you is the cause of my trouble.'

" 'How so ?'

" 'I shan't tell you.   You told me I said too much the other day.'

" 'Either too much or not enough was what I said.   Tell me all you have to say, and then you will not have said too much. Tell me, dear Mary,' I added, squeezing her plump little hand, thinking I might perhaps get at the truth by a little pretence of affection.   Clearly Mary meant to have a flirtation, and thought it was commencing.

" 'Don't squeeze,' she said, coquettishly. 'If you love me, tell me so, but don't squeeze, or I shall scream.'

" I know the ways of girls pretty well, so

I squeezed a little harder; and Mary did *not* scream.

"'Mary,' I continued, in my most lover-like whisper, though I felt considerably more like a confessor than a Lothario, 'I shall not love you, I will not call you my friend unless you tell me exactly how far this affair has gone between Percy and yourself. I may be able to help you out of any difficulty—may have the power to make him marry you; but you must tell me all first.'

"Then she told me all; told me the old commonplace story of deceit and treachery; the almost unromantic history of a confiding child and an unprincipled man. I was listening so intently to her story that I had no ears for the catlike tread of a man behind us. It was quite dark now too, so I did not see him until he was close upon us. I had just said to her—

"'Good heavens! And you are in this man's choir—you sing in his church on Sundays, do you not?'

" ' Yes, she does—or rather she did,' said a voice behind us, which I knew was Percy's, ' for from this night she will do so no longer. Loose her arm from yours and let go her hand.'

" ' What are you going to do with her?' I asked, as I mechanically obeyed.

" ' Going to do? What would any clergyman do but take the poor child home to her mother, away from a godless libertine —a married rake?'

" After what I had just heard, I was so startled by the fellow's consummate impudence that I was positively dumbfounded.

" ' Stand aside, will you?' he proceeded, gaining courage from my silence. ' Attempt to force yourself upon us as you did once before, and I will call the police directly we get into the town. You have beguiled this thoughtless girl into a course which will cost her the position she holds at my church, and involve her mother in still more hopeless poverty than before. Let that suffice. Come with me, Mary.'

"The girl went with him unhesitatingly. I said to her—

"'Can you, after what you have told me, walk one step with that man?'

"'What have you been telling him?' he asked, his face livid with suppressed anger.

"'Nothing.'

"'Nothing! What does he mean, then, by his taunts?'

"'I cannot tell, Mr. Llewellyn. I foolishly consented to walk with Mr. Lund, instead of coming to practice; but I am quite ready to go with you, and to promise both you and my mother never to speak to Mr. Lund or any gentleman again.'

"I could see Percy did not believe a word of what the palpable little fibber said; but it suited his purpose to pretend that he did; so he stopped short and said to me—

"'You hear what the girl says. Now have the goodness to choose which way you will go, and we will take the opposite direction. We simply want to be relieved of your company. Is it not so, Mary?'

" ' Yes, Mr. Llewellyn.'

" If I am not vastly mistaken, Mary gave me a smirk over Percy's shoulder as I took the road by the church, leaving them to turn on their heels and go home by the way I had come, past the Fishponds and under the dark lane beneath to the wood. The last sound I heard was the girl's silly giggle ringing through the quiet night air.

" I passed down the long mean street of the East Zoar suburb, then took a turn or two in the cathedral green, looking up at the window of my old lodging, and still musing on how the times had changed. I fear, too, my cogitations had a misanthropic air; for I meditated on the unwisdom of interfering in other people's love-affairs, and speculated on the exceedingly small chance there was of setting a light, frivolous girl right, when she made up what little mind she had to go wrong. The clock struck ten whilst I was thus moralizing; so I went hurriedly home, for I had to be up and off early next morning on my Arcadian tour.

"'What have you pegged up that ill-favoured glove over the chimney-piece for?' said Elsie. 'Is it a gage of battle, or to remind me of my duty? In the latter case it is unnecessary; for see, here is a new pair for you.'

"'I peg it up there not for your sake, but my own, dear Elsie, to remind me how our first married quarrel resulted from my fractious temper, which even a trifle like that could ruffle.'

"'Good; confession is halfway towards amendment, as Mrs. Fane would say. By the way, Alec,' added Elsie, 'if you have not sealed up your letter to her don't do so. I shall find the time hang heavily when you are gone, so shall very probably add a long postscript before the London mail goes out.'

"Then I told her of my ill success with Mary Baker; and we both agreed that, when I came back from my few days' excursion, it would be better for me to call on the mother and give her a word of warning. And now, good-night. Elsie shall fulfil her design and finish this in a postscript.

" P.S. (by Elsie)—I can scarcely find a moment to tell you the terrible event that has happened ; but it is quite necessary you should be informed, for I do not know in what trouble it may not innocently involve us.

" I thought the town seemed in an unusual state of commotion this morning. People were hurrying hither and thither, and from early morning there was quite a crowd gathered a little higher up the street than our house. We have not had much heart to show ourselves in public since my father's troubles came upon him ; so it was later than it would else have been, perhaps, when my mother came into my room, and exclaimed—

" ' Who would have believed that such a thing could ever have happened in Zoar, Elsie ? There has been a murder during the night.'

" ' A murder !'

" ' Yes, or suicide, but it seems more likely to turn out the former.'

" ' Who is dead ?'

" ' Poor pretty little Mary Baker.'

" ' Mary Baker—dead !' I rejoined ; and felt my mouth and throat growing dry and parched as I uttered the words.

" ' Yes, drowned in the Fishponds. They had been scouring the country for her as she did not come home after practice last night, and found the body this morning. It will kill her mother, poor old soul.'

" ' My dear mother, what is this you tell me ?' I shuddered as I said ' Mary Baker never went to practice last night.'

" ' How in the world do you know that ?' my good mother asked, opening her eyes as though for the moment she thought I had something to do with the poor girl's untimely fate.

" ' Alec was with her at practice time.'

" ' With her—where ?'

" ' In the Fishpond Fields.'

" ' What, in the name of mercy, for ?'

" Then I spoke to my mother as one woman speaks to another, and told her how Alec had been trying to recal Mary from the wrong course into which she had been beguiled by Percy. And then, too, there once more came across my mind a flash of that terrible consciousness to which I have before alluded. She did not believe what I was telling her. She thought Alec had other motives for meeting Mary at the Fishpond Fields. She thought Alec had murdered her, and that I was screening him. She did not utter a word of all this; did not consciously convey it by a look, but I knew that it passed through her mind. I could not but realize that her conviction was a common sense one, and that what she thought, other people would soon begin to say.

" In her case previous prejudice against Alec combined with the implicit faith she still had in all that pertained to the family of Edward Llewellyn. She believed but too readily that Alec was with Mary Baker; but she did not believe that Percy had subsequently discovered them, and taken the girl away with him.

"'Mother!' I said, 'do not look so incredulous. Do you think I am not telling you the truth?'

"'I am sure you mean to tell me the truth, dear Elsie; what the dark secret is God and the guilty ones only know.'

"'But does anybody else share your dreadful suspicion? Oh, if Alec were only here to clear himself!'

"'I fear his sudden departure will look most suspicious of all. No; nobody has as yet connected his name with this event; for recollect you and I alone know that he saw the poor girl last night.'

"'Percy knows it.'

"'And no doubt generously holds his tongue until compelled to speak. Let us do the same.'

"'I shall do nothing of the kind. My

reticence will look as though I suspected him. He left the girl with Percy Llewellyn. On him, then, lies the onus of accounting for her fate. Where is he? Has he told all he knows? Father,' I continued—for my father came in at this juncture—'what is all this? Has the poor girl destroyed herself, or——'

" ' Been murdered, beyond a doubt. There are signs of a terrible struggle on the banks of the pond ;' and then my father too looked at me with that strange meaning look which it was my torture not to be able to misunderstand.

" ' Is anybody's name mentioned ?' I asked. ' For pity's sake tell me.'

" ' It would be unkind not to tell you, Elsie, that Alec's name is very freely mentioned—not as having made away with the girl ; they have not come to that *yet*, but as the only one who can possibly give a clue to her fate.'

" ' One—but not the only one. Percy was with her after Alec left her.'

"'The people do not seem to understand that, and I have not seen Percy or Moddle. They have been up all night helping in the search, and are now conveying the body home.'

"'If, as they say, Alec was the last person with her, why did they not come to him first of all to be put on her track?'

"'Why indeed?'

"'It would have looked like suspicion,' urged my mother. 'No doubt Percy felt a delicacy——'

"'Mother'—I could not help replying harshly and unkindly, I fear—'you will just drive me mad. You seem resolved to suspect nobody but poor Alec who is not by to defend himself. I tell you I know everything he knows. I sent him myself to keep that appointment with the poor girl. I know the damning revelations she made about Percy, and the motive he had for silencing her——'

"'Who is prejudging the case now, Elsie?' said my mother.

" ' I am not prejudging it. I am simply defending my absent husband ; but he must be absent no longer. I will go and fetch him myself. I wish he had never gone on this wildgoose newspaper business.'

" ' So do I, from my heart,' rejoined my father. He alone seemed desirous that Alec might exonerate himself. I could see still that my mother did not believe in the reason I assigned for Alec's meeting Mary. She thought I had been deceived.

" When I reviewed the chain of evidence against Alec, I own my heart sank within me. He was with the girl at nightfall. No doubt many persons saw them ; for he had no motive for concealment, and she was far too imprudent to take any precautions. Such a sight would be sure to awaken the curiosity of the Zoar gossips, and perhaps revive the damaging reports against Alec. Clearly people had been talking. Percy was at his choir practice, expecting Mary there. Even if he had been seen with her it would provoke no comment, for he often took her home by the nearest road across the Fishpond Fields. He had actually discovered her with Alec; and with whom she last was rested only on the words of the two men themselves. Of course I knew Alec was telling the truth—knew what was still more to the purpose, the base motive Percy had for wishing the poor girl out of the way. Perhaps he had heard the whole of her confession to Alec.

"Naturally I believed Alec, but *my mother thought I was being deceived.* She sat there with her calm grey eyes fixed on me as though she could read all that was passing through my mind, and expected me to come round to her opinion by-and-by. Shall I confess that the demon of unbelief did for a moment occupy my mind? Had I been deceived? Were my father and mother and the Zoar gossips right? Was Alec a dangerous man? Had he shown himself in his true colours at last?

"The black thought passed away so immediately, and was succeeded by such thorough confidence in my dear husband, that it would be an injustice to him if I did not chronicle its transient presence. It was literally the devil leaving me, and then the angels coming and ministering to me. I have got to know Alec so well now; I can see so clearly down beneath the surface of his not very transparent nature, that I make allowances for any appearances which seem against him. Other people do not do this. They rate him at his worst, and then this angers him so that he defies them, and determines to brave public opinion—foolishly, perhaps, for the odds are very long ones against an individual under such circumstances.

"There was now an increased commotion in the little street, and I was going to the window to see what it meant, when my mother, who was gazing out, put me back with her hand, and said—

"'Don't look, Elsie. They are bringing home the body.'

"'I am not afraid to look, mother,' I replied; and I peered out too, and saw the crowd standing awe-stricken around the little milliner's shop. It was that strange murmur which runs through a number of people at any crisis I heard just now, and this was succeeded by as significant a silence. They seemed holding their very breath now, and not a few bared their heads as the police carried the poor child on a stretcher, covered with such rough integuments as they had been able to find on the spot, and at a moment's notice.

"Foremost among those who followed the rough bier were Percy and Mr. Moddle. Percy was almost officious in his attentions, which was quite unusual for him, his ordinary manner being very reserved. I flattened my face against the window-pane, watching him with a strange fascination, until he passed into the little shop, and the door closed behind him. I pictured him face to face with the bereaved mother, and could not help saying to myself—

"'Is it possible he killed her?'

" Was there no hope ? It seems strange
to use the word ' hope ' in such a combination—but was there no possibility that it
was a case of suicide ; or that some marauders, and neither of those two with whom
she was last seen had deprived the girl of
life ?

" I knew exactly where I could find
Alec—at a little country village some
twenty miles off, which he was going to
make his headquarters, and stump the
vicinity for the purpose of getting data as
to the condition of the agricultural labourers.
I would, of course, go off to him at once,
and warn him of his perilous position.
Long before nightfall we could be back
again, and he would have given all the re-
quisite explanations. I would make him
forthwith cancel all his plans for those
ridiculous articles, and keep close by my
side until these difficulties were surmounted.
When I shall ever resume my work with
dear Amy, I am sure I cannot tell.

" I left my mother sitting grimly at the

window, and my father beginning to embrace his cranium once more; such being the characteristic action of each when anything worried them. For myself, I would dress hastily, and catch the very next train. I was nearly ready to start when I heard heavy footsteps ascending the stairs, and in a minute or two, following closely upon a loud rap at my door, Percy and Moddle entered the room, abruptly followed by the police inspector, and a constable, my father and mother bringing up the rear, and old Hannah half-scared, lingering quite in the distance. I had no time to protest against the intrusion, before Percy said—

"'I am sorry thus to break in upon you, Elsie; but it was absolutely necessary for the police to come, and I thought you would like to have some friends by, at the same time——'

"'Friends!' I ejaculated.

"'The inspector will act with all delicacy, and I am sure you will afford him every facility. Of course all this is purely formal. You have heard of poor Mary Baker's sudden death.'

"'What does he want? What do you want?' I asked, as calmly as I could.

"'I want to see the clothes Mr. Lund wore last evening, ma'am,' said the inspector, Percy having now fallen into the background. 'He has gone out of town, I am told.'

"'He has gone as far as Shapcott only, and I am going to fetch him back at once.'

"'And the clothes.'

"'He has them on still.'

"'Everything?'

"'Everything, I believe; but I must really look to be quite sure.'

"'Do so, please.'

"I obeyed, and left them in the bedroom, while I passed to Alec's dressing-room, the constable, however, keeping his eye on me all the time, while the inspector talked to Percy and Moddle.

"'Here is his hat, I see. He has worn his wide-awake,' I said. 'With that single exception he has on him everything he wore last night.'

"'You'll excuse me, ma'am,' continued the inspector; 'but about his gloves.'

"'He had one only last night,' I replied, recollecting our little quarrel. 'There it is, over the chimney-piece.'

"'So I see, ma'am. Constable,' he continued, 'hand me here that glove that was found beside the Fishpond. This seems the fellow to it.'

" As I live it was Alec's missing glove!

"'Where do you say that glove was found?' I asked, feeling my very lips grow white.

"'By the pond, this morning.'

" The doubt never recurred to my mind, not for a moment, I could swear it; but to all the bystanders that evidence was, I could see, conclusive. Percy's face wore an expression of fiendish malignity. Moddle's was an excellent reproduction of it. My mother's countenance grew rigid as stone, and even my father had lost hope. I could see all this at a glance, and began to fear I should faint. I kept my consciousness, however, by a violent effort, and said—

"'You have got all you want now. Let me go to my husband.'

"There was a movement on the part of the police which I could not understand; but they seemed to stand between me and the door.

"'You must pardon it, dear Elsie,' said Percy, in his most insinuating manner, 'but the police will have to go too, probably to go with you; but we will accompany you.'

"'We—who?'

"'Mr. Moddle and myself.'

"'Father, you must come with me and protect me from the machinations of these men—I do not mean the police, but these so-called friends. I see the devil's part they are playing. This is their revenge. You know the cause they have; and I know the cause one of them had to wish the poor girl out of the way. She told Alec last night——'

" 'Let me advise the lady not to say anything about last night, or to waste words at all,' observed the inspector. 'She had better go to Mr. Lund at once. We will not force our company upon her; but we must go too.'

" 'I would rather you went with me,' I replied. 'I am so thoroughly certain all will be cleared up directly you see my husband, that I shall be glad for as many as possible to accompany me, and witness my triumph over these two conspirators. I only stipulate that my father shall be by my side.'

" We set out in a body to walk to the station; and really there were as many people to look at us as there had been to stare at poor Mary's body. The general impression, I fancy, was, that in Alec's absence I had been tried and found guilty, and was being led off to execution then and there. The Zoar public are very uninformed as to the nature of judicial proceedings, though Zoar is an assize town too.

" At the station the police found my

information correct. Alec had booked to Shapcott by the parliamentary train, and set off reading his paper, the booking-clerk said, in such a calm free-and-easy manner, that he was quite sure *he* had not even heard of the occurrence. Alec is a favourite with all these people; and I was shocked to hear the very alacrity with which they began, if I may so say, to 'take sides,' just as though he were already on his trial, and they were discussing the pros and cons of the circumstantial evidence, and the chances for and against conviction.

"The most mysterious element so far, was the second glove. How that could have come to be by the Fishpond was more than I could guess.

"It was, as you may imagine, a melancholy journey enough; but I was buoyed up by the certainty of success at the end. It was very possible that Alec may have started on his bucolic excursions; but I was determined not to rest until I had found him; indeed the police would save me that trouble, had I been disinclined to take it on my own account. They considerately allowed my father and myself to occupy a different carriage from the one they rode in; but directly we alighted at Shapcott, they were by our side. I had no address to give them, as Alec was to write and inform me of his whereabouts; but it was such a little roadside place that the arrival of a stranger would be an event, and Alec would be bound to introduce himself to the station-master. The inspector and that official were at once in earnest conference; indeed I could perceive that the telegraph had already been at work, so that we were expected, and our business known.

"I am sorry to tell you that I forgot my strong-mindedness, and acted like what my good mother terms a 'thorough woman,' that is, I fell flat on the platform in a fainting fit when the inspector came to me, and said, somewhat abruptly—

"'Mr. Lund is not here, ma'am, nor has he been. In fact, not a single person has alighted at the station to-day, until we did so.'

"When I came to myself the police had gone, and Percy and Moddle with them. My father was sitting in the waiting-room of the station, holding his poor head, and looking in the most wobegone condition at me as I lay stretched on three uncompromising chairs by way of a couch.

"'They have gone to search for Alec,' he said, 'and there is nothing for us to do but go home and wait.'

"If the journey down was melancholy, what shall I say of the return? I have no doubt all will be cleared up by to-morrow's post; but in the meantime, hope deferred makes the heart sick indeed."

CHAPTER III.

DE PROFUNDIS.

DEAR MRS. FANE,—As I am not quite sure that you will remember even my name, though Alec tells me he has had occasion to mention it to you several times, let me just introduce myself to you by saying that I am, at this moment, I hope the best, and believe almost the only friend the Lunds have in Zoar. I am the precentor of the cathedral, and former college friend of Alexander Lund. If I except our good Dean and Mr. and Mrs. William Llewellyn, I really believe I may say I am the only person to stand between these good persecuted people, and a world which seems, for the moment, up in arms against them. Alec himself is, as I shall show you, not in a position to write to you;

and his wife, who has until this time borne up like a heroine, has broken down at last. I am writing by their request, almost at their dictation; therefore this letter is really Alec's letter to you. I had even debated whether I should not write it in the first person, and sign it by his authority with his name instead of my own. I do not adopt this course, because I do not wish to foist upon my friend the inevitable short-comings of what will follow. Lund is accustomed to write in narrative and descriptive style; I am not. My life here is a very placid and some would think a monotonous one. I never preach, and seldom write, therefore have grown considerably out of practice with my pen; and you will, I am sure, have occasion to make all sorts of excuses for shortcomings in these epistles which I have promised to indite to you. I presume on your assurance that you will do so, and proceed to lay before you the present state of my poor friend's surroundings.

" As I sit down to open the correspondence, I am conscious of doing so with the fullest confidence that all will come right, and very shortly too. They tell me that some sort of plan has been formed to weld these detached notes and letters into a regular serial story. If I for one moment thought that I should have to keep the interest alive from this point, which I understand to be somewhere in the second volume, right to the end of the third, I should lay down my pen in despair, frankly confessing myself unequal to the task. Alec is certainly 'under a cloud,' but I fancy I can see even now the silver lining in it.

"The most difficult and painful part of my task so far has been to remove from the mind of Elsie—I have begun to call her so, and she says it will be natural for me so to write of her to you—something very like a doubt of her husband's innocence. When she returned, weary and dispirited, with Mr. William Llewellyn, after their fruitless expedition in search of Alec, and leaving the police on his track, the circumstantial evidence did indeed seem strong against him; and if I had not known Lund as well as I do, I might have doubted him perhaps for a moment: but I do know that, with the supremest disregard of the convenances, and with an awkward habit of always showing himself in the worst possible light, he is at bottom a good and true—ay, a deeply religious man. Elsie tells me I can say this to you, for you know it too.

" She sent for me that terrible night, and told me in so many words of their failure to find Alec.

" 'You are his friend,' she said, 'and into your hands I commend his interests. See the Dean, and act as he advises. I frankly tell you I have—we have all of us—lost heart.'

" I said some of the stupid commonplaces one does say under such circumstances, and she proceeded—

" 'The damning evidence of that second glove found at the scene of the murder, and

Alec's divergence from the plan he proposed in the morning, have been too much for me. I will not say I doubt him—I do not ; but I cannot for the moment write to his friend with that supreme consciousness of his innocence, and full assurance of his future clearance, that I should like to convey, and which perhaps you can convey to her.'

" I assured her I could and would. Hence, behold me engaged in the capacity of his advocate and your correspondent.

" Our poor friend was brought back to Zoar in custody of the police, the same night as his wife and her father returned, and he at once sent for me. I seem to be elevated all of a sudden into quite an important personage. Everybody thinks of me, and finds me necessary for somebody else's interests. Hitherto I have been essential to nobody's well-being but my own. He explained to me at once what the police cautioned him against making clear to them—namely, the change from his proposed route. He got a newspaper, as we had been informed, and in it read of some agricultural labourers' meeting in a different direction from that which he had purposed taking. He determined, therefore, to sacrifice his Shapcott ticket, and make straight for the scene of action at once. This the police might have learnt, and did afterwards learn at the junction of the two lines, one going to Shapcott, and the other to Easton, where Alec was subsequently arrested on a warrant with which the executive were provided. Both the coroner's jury and the magistrates have, I regret to say, found primâ facie grounds for deeming him guilty of this poor girl's murder. Percy Llewellyn and Moddle make no secret of their satisfaction; indeed, have been indecently prominent in every examination of the accused, and active in raking up evidence against him. I rejoice to tell you, however, that the assizes are held very shortly here, so that the period of suspense will be short; and I, for one, cannot allow myself to have the slightest doubt of the result. The feeling among the townspeople, and even the police, is strongly in the same direction as my own, and even Alec himself is tolerably sanguine. Sheppard, the solicitor, has retained two of the best men on the western circuit, and will not hear a word of doubt as to the verdict.

" ' It is undoubtedly a strong case of circumstantial evidence,' he repeats to me over and over again; 'but I hold in my hand a clue to the most important links in the chain—one that I must not divulge or hint at even to you, and about which I have studiously closed your friend's mouth; in fact, he does not fully know it himself. I only bid him tell you and his wife that I have the most triumphant refutation of all suspicion ready to hand; and that I shall not be satisfied with simply rebutting this charge, I shall make it recoil on those who have in a great measure concocted it. I would not,' he adds, ' on any account have had the finding of the coroner's jury, or the magistrates other than it was. Had an open verdict been returned, your friend would have always had an ugly suspicion resting on him. As it is, he will be put on trial for his life, and come out of court, proved by a jury of his peers, not only an innocent, but an injured man.'

"Thus far, at Alec's own request, Elsie and he have not met. He said to me at the very first, it was impossible but that his wife and her family should share the general impression, that the evidence against him was irrefutable. Until he could embrace them all with clean hands he would keep aloof from them—it was so he himself phrased it—altogether.

"Outwardly he bears up with the utmost bravery under this terrible ordeal; but his incarceration is telling visibly upon him, and at times his spirits give way.

"'I must be,' he said to me just now, 'like Eugene Aram, "equal to either fortune," for we cannot disguise it that the trial may go against me. Thank God, not so much for my sake as for Elsie's, the period of waiting is short, and I have good hope of the issue; but in the meantime I feel in the position of a dying man. I have had, as you know, a bad character here; why I cannot imagine, and never condescended to inquire; but I am not conscious of ever having willingly wronged a living soul. My religious ideas have not been those of what are called right-thinking people; and for some time—long before this misfortune came upon me—I have been asking my conscience whether I have not in this respect done wrong rather to myself than others—whether I have not wilfully understated to myself the convictions which I really did entertain. But,' he said, kind good fellow as he is, 'I weary you with this, Briggs. You will think I am already adopting the regular jail-bird model-prisoner kind of whine, and talking to you as though you were the chaplain.'

"'Not at all, Lund,' of course I replied. 'I am only too glad to hear you speak as you do. I have often wished you would open out a little to me on these topics; but have, of course, felt a delicacy in beginning the conversation.'

" Alec at this point did me the honour of calling me an old brick, which, I know, according to his form of speech, is a very high encomium indeed. He did more than this, however; he enlightened me as to what has always been an enigma to me—namely, the state of his mind on religious matters, in the modification of which, he assured me, my dear madam, you had played a conspicuous part. He had never doubted what he rightly calls the great fundamentals of all religion, the existence of the Divine Being, and continued life succeeding so-called death.

" ' This,' he said, ' I consider incomparably superior to all else; these are the grand fundamentals on which every superstructure of religion or morality must be built up; and I am thankful to say I never for one instant found myself doubting these. All the deductions from these—all the human element in religion—I have considered, and still consider I had a right to accept or reject. For all I require some proof—some test—the grand criterion of all being, " By their fruits ye shall know them." Sometimes they seemed to me to answer but slenderly to such a test. But the others are innate ideas. I want no logic to tell me that God is, and that I shall live after death.'

" He did not seem to expect a reply, though he paused; so I was silent, and after awhile he proceeded—

" ' Perhaps I have needlessly set myself in opposition to some of the prejudices of my neighbours. I have had mine ; why should they not have theirs ? Why should I have gone about treading on people's corns ?'

" ' Don't speak of yourself in the past tense yet, Alec,' I suggested.

" ' I am thinking of myself in the past tense, and speaking to you, Briggs, as I think. These four narrow walls serve to force me in upon myself, and I speak as though I were some one else moralizing over my gravestone.'

"'Don't be downhearted, there's a dear old boy.'

"'I am not downhearted,' he answered, very sadly. 'If it were not for Elsie, I should care little how this matter turned out; for I have no one—never, to my knowledge, had any one but her, to feel an interest in me. Thoroughly conscious of innocence, I could calmly submit to be the victim of this devil's trick those two men are playing on me.'

"'Tell me,' I whispered, 'do you really believe Percy did this deed?'

"'I have not the smallest doubt of it; nor the faintest hesitation in saying that he contemplates a second murder in making me suffer for what he has done. I hold—that is, my advisers hold—triumphant evidence on this point, but whether that evidence will satisfy a British jury is quite another matter. I *think* it will; but there is, as you know, proverbially, an element of glorious uncertainty in the law. It may yet go against me.'

" ' We must hope for the best.'

" ' I do for the most part; but every now and then the atmosphere of this horrible place gets into my constitution and over-powers me for the moment.'

" ' Will you not change your mind and see Elsie ?'

" ' Does she wish it ?'

" ' I think so.'

" ' But you are not sure; I do not believe she does. I feel it will be far better for both of us not to meet until the ordeal is over.'

" ' Why not tell her the evidence you say you possess ?'

" ' I am pledged to secresy. An in-discreet word or look may spoil all. My escape, recollect, is not everything. We want to bring the real offender to justice.'

" ' But if— —'

" ' Yes; if I fail to do this, then I can

only swear to Elsie, as here once more I swear to you, that I am free from all complicity in this crime. I left Mary with Percy, as I have told you, and saw nothing of her afterwards, heard nothing but her merry laugh at my expense when I turned tail and departed alone. Do you believe this?'

"'From my soul I believe it, Lund.'

"'Tell me if you have the slightest doubt.'

"'Not a doubt; no. I am puzzled about the glove, it is true——'

"'And for the explanation of that you must await the trial. Now go straight from me to Elsie, and try to convey to her the conviction you say you feel.'

"'You believe I do feel it, don't you?'

"'Well, yes, I do now. Try and make her do the same.'

"I go to him every day between services, and the Dean has also visited him on several occasions. We are most pleased to see that, as the time approaches for the winter assizes, his spirits seem to brighten, and he scarcely entertains a doubt as to the issue of the trial so far as he is concerned. We have more trouble with his wife. Her hopes seem to sink in proportion to his elation. I do not think she doubts him more—though I believe there *is* a lingering doubt in the background affecting her almost unconsciously to herself. But our attention has been for a moment almost diverted from Alec by a new misfortune, or rather series of mishaps.

" In the first place, the house and business have been sold. With a forced sale, and the family under a cloud, I need not say that a slender sum only was realized, not nearly enough to pay the outstanding debts. The consequence is the poor old people have had to go into lodgings, where they are maintained entirely by Elsie. Alec had some small sums owing to him from the different newspapers, and these have been drawn to provide for their daily necessities. The rest is supplied by Elsie, and as she is not working at present, it is a mystery to the Zoar people where the funds come from. *It is no mystery to me!* God bless you for it, dear madam. The knowledge I have seems to make us friends at once, though I have never looked on your face, and perhaps never shall.

" 'I suppose the next thing my affectionate brothers will do,' said Mr. William Llewellyn to me, ' will be to adjudicate me a bankrupt. That is about the only link wanting in the chain of my misfortunes now.'

" ' Your brothers, do you say ?'

" ' Yes; Sam has been haunting me like a shadow. Edward keeps in the background, but I fear mischief from Sam.'

" ' Then may I ask you, my dear sir, is your belief as to the family respectability shaken in some of its clauses ?'

" He said nothing, but looked furtively in the direction of his wife, as though he would like to speak out but dared not.

" Mrs. William Llewellyn is generally one of the quietest and most undemonstrative of her sex ; one of those women we are apt to set down as nonentities, because they *are* quiet and undemonstrative; and I do not think that, prior to this occasion, although my visits have been rather frequent of late, I had heard her speak a hundred words. She always left the talking to other people, though she acted like a heroine when the occasion required, and not only so, but generally managed to have her own way in any domestic matters about which there was a difference of opinion. I have heard that these quiet women generally do ; but I am, as you know, a bachelor, and therefore cannot be expected to know much about the manners and customs of the fair sex. I was considerably astonished, however, by hearing Mrs. William Llewellyn suddenly and at some length deliver the following very pronounced opinion—

" 'I have held my tongue long enough,' she said—' too long some people tell me; but I am going to speak out now. You need not look at me any more, husband, when the family respectability is called in question. I don't believe in it any longer.'

" If she had suddenly abjured Christianity and confessed herself a ' 'vert' to the Mahometan faith or Buddhistic form of belief, she could scarcely have staggered us more than she did.

" 'Not only so,' she continued, ' but I have come to the very opposite conclusion, that these two brothers of yours, William, are just about two as great rascals as ever went abroad through some flaw in the legislation; and as for Percy—well, he is worthy of his origin. That's all.'

" 'My dear mother,' said Mrs. Lund, ' what has so suddenly changed your opinion ?'

" ' The change has not been sudden, Elsie, that is where it is. If this conviction had come suddenly, I might have doubted it; but it has come so gradually and I have so shut my eyes and stopped my ears to it, and still it would come, that I must be an infidel to doubt it. I can't tell you how I know it, but I do know that Percy killed that poor girl, and is now trying to kill Alec.'

" ' Bless you, mother,' exclaimed poor Mrs. Lund, 'for at last declaring your belief in my husband's innocence !'

" ' At last ! You wouldn't have had me declare before I did believe it, would you ? I don't believe it now—I know it.'

" Then Mr. Llewellyn took courage, too, to say that he knew the same. Gradually, and bit by bit, he told us the evidence had been forced in upon him that Edward was not exactly the good kind brother he had tried very hard to believe him to be. Sam's religion had blinded him, he informed us, for a long time ; but he had ceased now to give the hallowed title of religion to that rhapsody of words into which he had got to see Samuel Llewellyn's creed resolved itself. Indeed, we were all in one marvellous quarter of an hour reduced to the most remarkably uncharitable state of consentaneity. One and all, we agreed that the Llewellyn family were a gang of conspirators, and Lund their victim. I cannot tell how rejoiced I was to witness this consummation so devoutly to be wished, though I suppose as a clergyman, I scarcely ought to say so.

"It was inexpressibly comforting to your good friend, Mrs. Lund, to feel that, as she said, they could at last act as one compact body in their counterplot. Her spirits seemed quite to revive, and she almost shared her husband's hopefulness, though not without intervals of depression. While we were talking, there came a ring at the bell, and Mr. Moddle was announced. He was accompanied by one Nicholls, a medical man, and an old school friend of Mr. William Llewellyn. The Angel and Evangelist had hoped to convert Mr. Nicholls to their faith, and I was rather glad to witness their arrival, for I thought it would draw off Mr. Llewellyn's thoughts, if only for a moment, from the one absorbing topic. The ladies withdrew before Mr. Moddle and his friend entered. They were in no mood to receive visitors, and Mr. Moddle was not in their favour. I remained, as I was rather curious to interview an angel.

"'We have come, William,' said Mr. Nicholls, with a good deal of bonhomie, 'to see whether you will take a drive with us. Moddle is going to accompany me in my rounds — which happen to be rather extensive to-day—and we thought an outing would do you good. Do you not think so, Mr. Briggs?' he asked, addressing himself to me.

"'By all means,' I replied. 'I should think it was the very thing to do Mr. Llewellyn good. He is very nervous.'

"'You find him so?'

"'I do indeed. He has been holding his head a good deal more than I like to see him,' I added, laughing at my host as I did so.

"'Yes, that holding the head,' interposed Mr. Moddle, 'is a very bad sign indeed;' and he looked significantly at the doctor.

"'Let me feel your pulse, William,' said

Mr. Nicholls, as he took his hand. 'Bless me! your blood is at fever heat, almost. Come and cool it in the fresh air.'

"It was a long time before they started, and in the interval, we went over pretty nearly all the clauses of the Irvingite creed, I should think. Mr. Llewellyn struck me as being a more pronounced adherent of that form of faith than Mr. Moddle himself. The revived apostolate, the resuscitation of prophecy, the unknown tongues, the imminence of the Second Advent—all these were forcibly put forward, and Mr. Llewellyn expressed his full belief in them. Mr. Moddle said little, and Mr. Nicholls nothing to commit himself. They seemed to me to be drawing out Mr. Llewellyn for my edification.

"'Come along,' said the doctor at last. 'You will scare Mr. Briggs if you say any more. He looks as though he thought us all lunatics now.'

"'You do think me mad on this point— an amiable monomaniac, don't you?' asked

Mr. Llewellyn, as he prepared to go for his drive.

"'Frankly, since you ask me the question, I do.'

"'Of course he does,' was the comment of the two; and off they went, leaving me to entertain Mrs. Llewellyn and Mrs. Lund.

"I was somewhat surprised, considering that Mr. Llewellyn was to be taken for a cooling drive, to find that they went in a closed carriage; and still more so, to see the vehicle stop a little way up the street to allow Percy Llewellyn to join the party inside, and Sam to mount the box. I did not say a word to the ladies, because I did not want to alarm them, but I feared mischief; and was not at all surprised to learn in the course of the evening that Mr. William Llewellyn had been driven off straight to the county lunatic asylum, and there detained on the strength of certain 'delusions,' attested by Mr. Moddle and the medical man, it being also added that I must hold myself prepared to substan-

tiate, if necessary, his precarious state of
mind.

"Now, of course, the cloven foot is
plain enough, and we none of us doubt for
one moment the dreadful conspiracy that
there is against these good people. Sheppard bids us be of good cheer; for, he says,
our enemies are taking rope enough to
hang them all. But in the interim they
are abroad, and our two unfortunate men
are in durance vile. I wish I were a little
more worldly wise, so that I could see my
way clear to get them out.

"Who could fancy that this was our dear
quiet stupid Zoar, where, once upon a time,
the smallest petty larceny was enough to
set the whole community chattering; and
here we have a murder and an abduction—
I can call it nothing else—both at once, to
regale ourselves with. The best of it is—
so Mr. Sheppard says—the people *do* talk,
and very freely and undisguisedly indeed,
about this last coup. There is always a
good deal of animus between the towns-

people and the cathedral folk, our good
Dean alone excepted, who is a favourite
with all; and Edward Llewellyn has always
tried, infructuously enough, as it happens,
to identify himself with the cathedral element, so that the townspeople look upon
this treatment of his brother as a direct
onslaught upon themselves.

"'Recollect, my dear sir and madam,'
said that most 'cute of lawyers, Sheppard,
to me and Alec's wife, 'the jury will be
empanelled from those very people who are
now wagging their tongues so freely. I
should feel pretty sure of my verdict even
without the marvellous evidence I am
holding back. Look at Moddle; he has
smelt powder and made off. The people
would have lynched him if he hadn't. They
look very much askance at Nicholls, though
they know he is a poor man, who has probably been well paid and has kept carefully
within the letter of the law and the limits
of professional etiquette. You will pardon
me if I quote a word or two of Latin, won't

you? " Quem Deus perdere vult priùs dementat." Edward Llewellyn must have been insane himself to interpolate this lunatic asylum trick at such a crisis. It insures our verdict ; and I would not for any amount of money have had things otherwise.'

"It is quite true Moddle has bolted. These people, it appears, have some regulations similar to that of the Jesuits, whereby they are bound to go at a moment's notice whithersoever the Pope sends them—the Pope in this case being represented by the apostolate. Well, the apostolate suddenly discovered—or Moddle gave it out so— that his angelic ministrations were required elsewhere ; so he has flitted.

" ' It's all very well for Mr. Sheppard to say he would not have had things otherwise,' observed Mrs. William Llewellyn ; ' but what of my poor husband ? Read that letter that I have received from him. Is that the letter of a lunatic ?'

"It was only a few melancholy lines, scribbled as soon as he had arrived at his destination; but I was fain to confess there were in it no symptoms that the writer was other than compos mentis.

"'But you said he was a lunatic,' suggested Mrs. Llewellyn.

"'In mere joke, and simply in reference to his Irvingite proclivities,' I replied.

"'It was only a little while ago that poor Alec was saying how prone we were to call everybody a lunatic who differed from us,' added Mrs. Lund. 'He little thought his words would shortly receive so pertinent an illustration.'

"At last the day of the trial has arrived; a bleak, damp, winterly day, that looks as though it were doing all it could to depress us. All the penny-a-liners, as you will have seen, speak of this as a cause célèbre—that is their constant phraseology—and the excitement is intense. I am waiting for the Dean who is to accompany me; and we both of us dined with the judges last night. I could not help looking with amazement at the one who is to try the criminal cases, as he sat sipping his wine calmly and complacently after dinner, thinking how the life of my dear friend—perhaps the lives and fortunes of all the little knot of friends that centre round Alec—might perhaps on the morrow, that is to-day, hang on the breath of that man's mouth. He is a first-rate lawyer, as you know; a college friend of the Dean's, and always ready—so the Very Reverend informs me—to strain a point on the side of mercy. He is not what they call a hanging judge.

"How horrible it sounds to use that word even in possible reference to Alec!

"Here is the Dean. I shall take these sheets with me into court, and just jot down what occurs, giving you only the salient points of the trial, posting the letter directly it is over, and leaving the newspapers to fill in the details. Let me premise that I am utterly ignorant of all judicial proceedings, never having been in court before in my life.

"When the jury was empanelled, Alec standing proudly, though with no symptom of bravado, in the dock, Sheppard gave me a secret but unmistakeably triumphant look as one by one the names were called over. To a man they were Alec's friends. If we had picked the panel ourselves we could not have had better men.

"Then the case for the Crown opened, and the prosecuting counsel calmly — I could not help confessing fairly—laid the whole of the damning evidence before the jury, dwelling of course most strongly on the fact that, as would be proved in evidence, Alec was the last person seen with the murdered girl, and that one of his gloves was found close to the spot where the crime was committed. He freely confessed that the evidence was purely circumstantial—it was seldom otherwise, for men did not commit murders in a crowd— and combated in advance the notion of absence of motive. He was not bound to assign a motive, but there was a very natural one, that would no doubt suggest itself to their minds. He dwelt upon it in details which I do not care to repeat here, but I could see that his words produced no effect. The faces of those twelve men were not intellectual, not expressive ones; but they told me that the wicked deduction did not find favour with those on whom poor Alec's life would by-and-by depend. He was bound, as an advocate, to put that view forward; but I wonder whether I was wrong—I fancied he could see that his theory carried no conviction with it.

"Then came the witnesses. The police deposed to the night-long search, and the finding of the body with signs of the death struggle on the bank of the pond. Next followed the discovery of the glove, and the identification of it as the missing one of the pair, and the circumstance of the other being pegged up over the chimney-piece in Alec's bedroom. The counsel for the defence made a point of that—that it was pegged up openly and undisguisedly, and so as to attract attention. The change of route next morning was put forward as a link in the chain of evidence, and quietly explained by a simple question on the part of Alec's counsel again. Then came the question, with whom was the murdered girl last seen in company?

"I am afraid I was conscious of a sort of admiration at the consummate way in which Percy Llewellyn stood there in the witness - box, and perjured his soul by swearing that he left Mary Baker with Alec. Both those men, the one at the dock, and the other in the box, were wonderfully calm and self-possessed; but Alec the more so of the two. It was a life-and-death struggle, more terrible than as though they were standing face to face in deadly combat, depending upon their thews and muscles as to which should die; most terrible of all, because Alec's lips were sealed, and he was bound to listen while the other tried to swear his life away.

"I feel quite sure now that when Percy

Llewellyn left the box he felt Alec was safe, and experienced the sensation of a halter round his own neck. May his prognostications be realized!

"Slowly, and mesh by mesh, as it seemed to me, the net was thus woven round our poor friend. The court adjourned late for luncheon, and then came the defence.

"The assertion as to Mary having been last seen with Alec was, the counsel suggested, assertion only. One man's mouth was closed, the other might be swearing what was false. The frightful reason he had for so doing could not, of course, be touched on. The medical evidence had only proved the poor girl's condition; but proved—or even suggested—nothing more —nothing as to whose door *that* crime might lie at. The glove was relied on as triumphant evidence that Alec was on the spot at the time of the murder. All Zoar held its breath—for pretty well all Zoar was in court—as the counsel, carefully prompted by Sheppard, called one of

Edward Llewellyn's clerks, the feebler of
the two lads who had been in attendance on
the day when the Dean and myself went
with Alec to the office. Had he ever seen
that glove before? He had. (Police and
lawyers' clerks never say 'yes' or 'no' in
the witness-box; but always 'I have,' or 'I
have not.' It sounds professional.) Would
he state when and where? He picked it
up on the occasion of Mr. Lund's calling
at the office, naming the day and hour.
What did he do with it? Simply put
it on Mr. Edward Llewellyn's table.
Did he draw Mr. Edward Llewellyn's
attention to it? He did not. He had
never seen it afterwards until it was in the
hands of the police; in fact, had forgotten
the circumstance of finding it; and could
not in the least explain why he put so
worthless an article on Mr. Llewellyn's
table, instead of in the coal-scuttle, or under
the grate; but he had a most distinct recollection that he did put it there, and there
left it.

"All this, which it takes me so short a time to write in my informal way, was slowly elaborated in painful detail, and with all sorts of technicalities of expression. There was a wordy war between the counsel as to no notice having been given of the line of defence to be adopted, and Alec's friends again augured favourably, from the fact that the judge in every case ruled on the side of the defence. His character for mercy was evidently peeping out.

"Alas, I must send off this instalment as an instalment only; for the shadows of the brief wintry day came down upon the little court before the speech for the defence was finished, and there was no hope that the judge would sum up until the morrow. So we had to do that weariest of all things— wait.

"But we waited confidently and with good hearts. There was no more despondency on Alec's account; we could only reserve our anxiety for Mr. William Llewellyn. Even Mrs. Lund quite lost all

symptoms of depression, for everybody congratulated her beforehand on the anticipated
issue of the morrow.

"'It seems impossible that to-morrow
this time he will be with us again,' she
said.

"'Not at all impossible, but certain,' replied Mr. Sheppard, who was by.

"'Scarcely certain.'

"'Yes, morally certain. That jury now
comfortably locked up at the Mitre Hotel
are not only twelve good men and true, but
—what is much more to the purpose—
twelve men committed beforehand to our
view of the matter.'

"I think I may venture to say none of
us slept that night; at least, from what I
know ex post facto, Alec himself was the
only one who yielded to the blandishments
of Morpheus. For myself, I retired per-
functorily to my lodgings, and the two
ladies made tremendous pretence of getting
a good night's rest. I must confess—and
they plead guilty to the same—that I was

consciously hypocritical, and passed the night advisedly in trying to picture poor Alec's terrible vigil. Poor Alec, I find, made a capital supper, turned in early and slept like a top. How constantly the romantic eludes our grasp under circumstances where we might expect its presence, and crops up under the most unlikely ones.

"The judge commenced his summing-up as soon as the court opened the next morning, and evidently was not inclined to forfeit his character for tempering justice with mercy from having 'slept upon' Alec's case. His résumé of the evidence was clear and lucid, but with an undisguised bias towards the accused. The question as to who was last with Mary Baker was, to say the least of it, not proven. Even this qualified assertion admitted the possiblity of perjury in the case of Percy Llewellyn, and if perjury, something worse; for it was evident either the prosecution or the defence had misrepre-

sented the proceedings on that fatal evening. The judge said as plainly as he could
say, without resolving himself into an advocate, that he did not believe the state-
ment put forward by the prosecution on
this point. The glove business was, he
told them, satisfactorily explained. The
missing glove had passed out of Alec's possession, and there was no evidence as to its
whereabouts, beyond the testimony which
left it on Mr. Llewellyn's table. There
was nothing, at all events, to show that it
ever reverted to its original owner, and
every presumption that it did not so revert.
Lastly came the important item of motive,
which in a case of purely circumstantial
evidence was not to be lost sight of. It
was quite certain, from the medical testimony, that somebody had an interest in
the poor girl being put out of the way, and
it was morally certain the accused was not
that person. Who it was they had not to
decide. They must keep out of their mind
everything that did not bear on that to

him, terrible alternative, the guilt or innocence of the accused.

"When the summing-up was finished, and the jury left to consider their verdict, the usual question was put to them, as to whether they wished to retire for that purpose. Under some circumstances, even when the verdict is a foregone conclusion, the jury have withdrawn pro formâ; but it was not so here. We were spared the misery of delay, at all events., A significant glance ran round the jury box; a single word was spoken, and the unanimous verdict given by the foreman, in reply to the judge's demand, 'Do you find the prisoner at the bar guilty or not guilty?'

"'Not guilty, my lord.'

"It was no use trying to restrain the applause. The little court rang with it; the judge protesting, the officers insisting, in vain. All sense of dignity, it might be said of decorum, was lost. The people fairly shouted, embracing judge, jury, and prisoner in one comprehensive salvo of congratulation. Those outside got the news, and took up the same strain. Zoar quite forgot its propriety; and Mrs. Lund and Mrs. Llewellyn knew the result long before I had rushed to tell them, and then rushed back and fetched Alec to bring the news himself. Sheppard and myself took him to the door of the humble lodging where his wife dwelt, accompanied by a crowd who pressed to shake him by the hand; and then we all left him, as we felt it would be unkind to break in upon the sacred joy of man and wife under such circumstances.

"I turned to go home, but was borne in quite another direction by the tagrag and bobtail of Zoar, who having had a taste of judicial proceedings, were inclined to try the case over again on their own account before the tribunal of Judge Lynch. They adjourned en masse to Edward Llewellyn's smug residence, and insured employment for the glaziers for some days by smashing all the windows. The few police

seemed mysteriously absent, so that the
marauders had it all their own way; and
when the executive did make their appearance, it was not for the purpose of
dispersing the rioters, who had already dis-
solved into fortuitous atoms on their own
account, but to arrest Percy Llewellyn on
suspicion of Mary Baker's murder. That
satisfied the mob's idea of retributive justice,
and they reassembled to see the parson led
forth ignominiously. In this they were
disappointed, however, for when the inspector and his myrmidons re-emerged from
Mr. Llewellyn's residence, the former so far
forgot official reserve, as to say to an
acquaintance—

"'Bolted!'

"It was too true. Percy had seen on
the former night what the issue of the trial
would be, and knew only too well the alternative that occurred to every mind as a
necessary one. If Alec Lund was innocent,
he must be suspected to be guilty. The
chances of anybody else having done the

deed were, as he no doubt realized in his lawyer-like mind, infinitesimal.

"The day succeeding the trial was a kind of levée for Lund. Mrs. Dean sat in state with Elsie (I have got to call her so now), and the Very Reverend and myself flitted in and out between services. The tide had turned, Alec was a dangerous man no longer, but an injured individual, a man with an unmistakeable grievance; and Zoar lost no time in making the amende honorable. Mrs. Grundy was quite in the minority.

"The great mistake made by the conspirators (I can call them so now without prejudicing matters), was the consignment of Mr. William Llewellyn to the lunatic asylum. They showed their hand too plainly. The trial was out of their discretion to bring about or avert. It was a strange piece of circumstantial evidence which they had, of course, used for their own purposes, and, in the instance of the glove, might or might not have forged.

But the onslaught upon poor Mr. William Llewellyn was what some people consider worse than a crime; it was a mistake—a bungle.

" To get a special meeting of the Visiting Justices, and procure the release of Mr. Llewellyn, was a short matter; and he is now at home again. Indeed, the family circle is now quite reunited, and all Alec talks of is retaliation. Mrs. Llewellyn's former spirit has so far returned that she prays him thus—

" ' Let bygones be bygones, Alec. Let things rest. Time will bring the offenders to justice.'

" ' But there is not the slightest reason, my good mother, why we should not second the efforts of Time in that respect. I deliberately propose to myself now one or two ends from which nothing or nobody will make me swerve : these are,' and he told them off on his fingers—' no rest for the sole of my foot until Percy Llewellyn stands in that dock where I have stood;

secondly, the restitution of the purchase-money for High Street and the whole of the shares of Topaz; and last, not least, perhaps, the forcible extraction from Aunt Rachel of all she knows about the Welsh estates.'

" Mr. Llewellyn smiled a smile of amiable incredulity, and his wife said, as plainly as looks could say, that she would like to let things remain as they now were; but Elsie went over to her husband's side now.

" 'I am no advocate of the lex talionis,' she said.

" 'Meaning, Elsie?' suggested her mother.

" 'Meaning the law of retaliation—the eye for the eye, and the tooth for the tooth; but simple reversion to the "as you were" position is not enough now. Justice, full justice, must be done. We must clear our-selves.'

" And the Dean, who was by when Elsie enunciated these Sibylline sentences, declared that Mrs. Lund was right.

" ' I shall feel it my duty,' he said, 'not to rest until I have seen Mr. Lund through with this. He has been, beyond a doubt, the victim of a very determined conspiracy indeed, and he must not rest until he has escaped from its meshes. I am sorry for Edward Llewellyn. He is a proud man, and I fear his son's misdeeds will humble that pride. But we must not let this sway us. That poor girl's blood cries to us from the ground. Nay, more, these good people here are not in the position they should be. For years they have suffered deprivation, and their losses must be repaired. I wonder where Sam Llewellyn is,' he added, with a gasp, as though a new idea had struck him, and he had got to the very bottom of the matter now.

" ' Sam,' answered Alec, 'has, I believe, really gone now on his projected Irish tour. It is no secret that the police have tracked the movements of uncle and nephew so far. The former went through South Wales to Holyhead, en route for Ireland, the latter sped by last night's mail to the metropolis, feeling safer, no doubt, with two or three million people around him, than here in Zoar, where he had come to be an object of such very unenviable notoriety.'

" ' We shall have him back very shortly.'

" ' Unless he manages his journey better than I did my Shapcott expedition,' said Lund, with a laugh. 'I never like to reckon too surely on the acuteness of the police. They are apt to desert us at our utmost need. Percy is equal to any detective in existence.'

" I wanted Mrs. Lund to finish off this letter, but she prefers that I should conclude what she is good enough to say I have so well begun and carried out. I hope you have been able to gather from these fragmentary epistles of mine something like the progress of events; but I have been launched unexpectedly into the onerous duties of a Special Correspondent at a very important crisis, and scarcely feel equal to the occasion.

"She will resume the thread of the narrative from to-morrow, and I shall retire modestly into the background again. I really feel as though this share in Alec's trouble has braced me up and done me good. Perhaps the existence of a minor canon in a cathedral town is apt to stagnate somewhat.

"It is beautiful to see Zoar settling down and becoming itself again. Assize week is always more or less trying, and this one has been, I need not say, exceptionally so. To have to sing the service before the assembled bench and bar on Assize Sunday is always a sore trial to me; and I was particularly glad to see my Lord's carriage, the High Sheriff with his javelin-men, and all the rest of the paraphernalia decamp and leave our little city to its accustomed calm.

"I cannot help, however, now I am fairly roused, speculating what the next event will be, for I feel sure things are only in an incipient condition yet. Alec Lund is not the man to sit down quietly under a series of wrongs like this. Indeed, though I am essentially a man of peace myself, I do not see how he could do so. He has the interests of others besides himself to consult.

" Do you know it makes me rather glad I am a cœlebs and a quiet precentor, when I see what comes of giving hostages to fortune, and going out into the busy world of men and women away from one's cathedral close and comfortable stall. Let me rest and be thankful."

CHAPTER IV.

AUNT RACHEL'S REVELATIONS.

F this were ever going to assume the form of a novel, my dear Mrs. Fane—and really there seems incident enough to warrant such a metamorphosis—the professors of the Gay Science would, immediately upon its publication, declare it to be the most inartistic thing possible. It pretty well began by giving my marriage with Alec, instead of saving me up to the end, putting him through all sorts of troubles to get me, and then awarding him my hand at the end of the third volume as the premium of distinguished merit. Again, the murder and trial, instead of being spread over a volume or two, were disposed of in a couple of chapters; the whole De Lunatico Inquirendo business in a few lines, and altogether the great things have been dwarfed and the little ones magnified. It's very nice doing one's own criticism beforehand; and I pause to ask myself, Is it not so that things happen in life? They do not arrange themselves, I mean, in three volumes like a novel, or three paragraphs like a leader or a sermon. They are apt to come spasmodically; and, for the life of me, I cannot see why, if we are to hold the mirror up to Nature, we should not represent them so.

"I was talking to Alec about this, and he was rather shocked at my literary heterodoxy. He said—

"'You seem, Elsie, jumping to the conclusion that the interest of our life history has culminated in my escape from durance vile. I don't think so. Events are but in embryo yet. I mean to have something much more interesting than marriages or murders before I have done with existence.'

"'Do you indeed? And what, may I

ask, is your special line of sensation-mongery?'

" 'I predicted events, did I not, while all in which we were concerned seemed to be and likely to remain as uneventful and plain-sailing as Zoar itself?'

" 'You did so, and therefore I ask you all the more anxiously what is the special line to be? You have exhausted matrimony and murder. What remains?'

" 'I think I won't tell you just now.'

" 'Because you can't,' I replied, tauntingly, 'any more than you could predict poor Mary Baker's drowning. It was only a happy coincidence.'

" 'I don't know much about the happiness of it,' Alec answered, with recollections of his incarceration and trial fresh upon him, no doubt. I felt quite repentant for my want of consideration in recalling his recent sufferings by my thoughtless remark.

" 'I am only resting on my oars just to get breath before I go in for the next sensation, which will, forensically speaking, shift the interest from the Crown to the Nisi Prius side of the Assize Court at Zoar. I shall certainly instigate a move in the matter of the Topaz Farm and the High Street business, if your worthy parents do not suffer from a relapse of family respectability.'

" 'I don't think there is much danger of that now.'

" 'Nor I. Their eyes must be pretty well opened by this time. I wonder whether Percy is caught,' he continued, 'or whether he will be clever enough to elude the hue-and-cry.'

" 'Percy is 'cute.'

" 'Cunning as a fox; and no doubt has made his preparations well beforehand. I should not be in the least surprised if he baffled us.'

" 'Don't you rather wish he may?'

" 'Speaking from my own individual and unregenerate standpoint, I should be inclined to say No! I have such a vivid recollection of my own escape from the infernal meshes he wound round me, that I should rather like him to feel what it is to be involved in them himself. On the life for life principle, Percy ought to swing. For the credit of the family, it might be as well perhaps that the gallows should not be quartered amongst its heraldic bearings; but I was so very near it myself that really the decoration seems quite familiar.'

" ' Would it not be better, even now, to adopt the policy I acted upon once—take the wings of the dove, flee away and be at rest ?'

" ' You took me as your dove on that occasion recollect, which will account for your readiness to flee, and subsequent sensation of rest.'

" ' We have enough—or can make enough —to live upon and keep the old folks. Let us go, and leave these people to Heaven and to those thorns that in the bosom lodge to prick and sting them.'

" ' No ! that I will not do,' answered Alec, quite sternly; 'and I don't believe,

10—2

Elsie, you want me to either. No, if you quote Hamlet to me, I will retort with Hamlet upon you. I am bound to revenge this foul and most unnatural murder.'

" 'Poor Mrs. Baker is willing to let her daughter's fate remain unsolved. She was only anxious you should escape. She would rather not know who was the murderer.'

" 'She is another of your long-suffering people who require to be goaded into a necessary and proper resentment. She knows in her heart who did this murder.'

" 'I believe she does; but she clings to the belief—avowedly, at least—that some other hand than Percy's did the deed. He was always so good and kind,' she says.

" 'Good and kind indeed. I wonder what Aunt Rachel would say about his goodness and kindness. I must get you to come with me and pump that old lady. In the natural course of things she can't last much longer, even with an annuity to keep her alive. I shall do a little auricular confession with her on the subject of certain family antecedents.'

" 'Touching the Welsh estates?'

" 'Touching those, among other matters. Why do you always smile when you name those estates?'

" 'Because I believe they exist only in Aunt Rachel's fertile imagination.'

" 'Anyhow let us go and hear about them. Psychologically, if in no other way, it will be interesting to examine into our patrimony.'

" 'We will go by all means.'

" We paid our proposed visit to the old lady, who since Aunt Phillis's departure seldom gets up. These apparently useless existences are a strange problem. Perhaps we shall solve it in this instance by utilizing Aunt Rachel as they do certain aged individuals in a right-of-way case.

" We found her sitting bolt upright in bed, in the most outrageously uncomfortable way, as far as one could judge; and as we had announced our intention of paying her

a visit, she was heavily attired in a re-
splendent cap and dressing-gown. There
was no difficulty in getting her on to the
topic of family affairs, for, since her niece's
death, she had felt a sort of taboo removed,
and could unbosom at pleasure, that is
when she had any listeners. Under ordinary circumstances her circle was limited
to a small girl of tender years, who formed
her sole retinue, and who, I am sure, if
she retained half she was compelled to hear,
must have known considerably more than
we ourselves as to the archives of our
family. Mrs. Baker, Aunt Rachel said,
was a cunning and uncivil woman. She
fled precipitately as soon as the old lady
began her long yarns, and this was a
grievous offence. The older Aunt Rachel
grows, the more long-winded she becomes ;
and stories which even on their first narra-
tion possessed but a slight interest for outsiders, lost that when they were repeated for
the hundred and fiftieth time. Our arrival,
therefore, was something like a godsend for

the old lady; and as soon as we had discussed what she always termed our 'dish of tea,' she launched forth to something like the following effect.

" 'Lloyd Llewellyn, that is my father, your great-grandfather you know, Elsie, lived at a place in Wales which, as far as I can pronounce it now, sounded like Mudwalla.'

"I began to make a little genealogical tree in my diary, and stopped her to ask what county she thought Mudwalla was in. She had no notion, and I asked Alec to run over the counties, not feeling quite confident of my own geographical powers. She could not remember, and I don't think had any very distinct idea that the Principality was divided into counties, or even into North and South Wales.

" 'Anyhow, my dears, Mudwalla must be in the map; but all I can tell you about it is, that it was an old rambling country place near a moderate sized town, the name of which has quite escaped me. It was more than a farmhouse and less than a castle, and your great-grandfather was one of those fine old country gentlemen who were not called squires, but were ten times more like them than many who are now-a-days.'

"'What we should call a gentleman farmer,' I suggested.

"'I don't know what you would call them, Elsie, and it don't matter, because there ain't any of them to call now. He was a fine, rich, freehanded, outspoken gentleman, as different as possible from your upstart nobodies who marry deaf wives, and would sell the little soul they have to dine with the Dean or the Bishop.'

"This back-hander at Edward Llewellyn seemed to do the old lady good, and she proceeded—

"'A fine handsome fellow I have heard my father was in his younger days. He must have been, for he was a splendid specimen of a man when I can remember him ; of course all the girls of the country-

side were in love with him. You young
folks can understand that, can't you?'

"'Yes, aunt,' said Alec; 'we know
something about that, just a little, don't
we, Elsie?'

"'Well, I'm thankful to say I don't,'
proceeded my aunt. 'Why people can't
let one another alone, I never could understand. It would have saved a world of
trouble in this case.'

"'Of course it would have saved a world
of trouble in one way,' I remarked, 'because
we should not, any of us—except Alec—
have been in existence; and he seemed
inclined to your way of thinking until he
met me. Well, auntie, of all these bonny
Welsh lasses, I suppose Lloyd Llewellyn,
your handsome father, chose one.'

"'Not exactly, my dear. That would
have saved some trouble too if he had
stopped short there, but he chose two.'

"'Two, aunt! How could that be?'

"'Well, when poor Phillis was alive, and
was a little bit cross—she did get cross

sometimes you know—she used to say that you could explain that, Elsie.'

" 'I, aunt? How so?' I inquired, though I found myself blushing in a way that endorsed the truth of the old lady's remarks.

" 'Yes, she used to say that you were following in your great-grandfather's steps by being engaged to Percy Llewellyn, and carrying on with your present husband at the same time.'

" At this Alec broke into a most unmannerly horse-laugh, which my aunt seemed to take as a compliment, and joined in heartily. For the life of me I could not see what there was to laugh at. When she had got it over, she went on.

" 'It was, I have been told, just another such a case as yours. In very early youth a match had been arranged between my father and his cousin in some very remote degree—Welsh cousins are often very remote — Susanna Dash. Susanna's estate adjoined ours at Mudwalla, and it was considered that the two together would make the young couple about the biggest people in the neighbourhood.'

"'County people, in fact,' I suggested, just to see whether I could beguile the old lady into fixing the whereabouts of my Welsh inheritance. She was not to be ensnared by means of topography, however.

"'When things are so artfully planned, they seldom turn out as we intended, I think. Providence seems to take a pleasure in crossing our calculations. It was so in this case. Fanny Morgan——'

"'That was Number Two, I suppose?'

"'That was Number Two—just like this big interloping lord and master of yours,' she continued. 'Fanny Morgan was the daughter of a small farmer on the Dash Estate, a pretty, apple-faced girl, like the poor creature who was killed,' she said, sinking her voice to a reverent whisper. 'There was no tragedy in this case, however, at least none that involved bloodshed or drowning in fishponds, or trials for murder, Alec; there was only what those people who have suffered from it tell me is just as bad—the slow death of being deceived, the murderous process of feeling all your love flung back upon you. It makes one glory in being an old maid, Elsie, when one thinks what one may possibly have escaped in this way.'

"'What those poor, dear heart-broken fellows Percy and Moddle must have felt in Elsie's case,' said Alec, resolved to turn the tables upon me, and to avenge his sex.

"'Be quiet,' I said. 'Go on, aunt.'

"'Susanna didn't die of consumption or throw herself into a fishpond. She did not even die young. She lived to be an old woman, and never uttered a word of reproach to my father. She sent for him one day, my mother used to tell me, and told him she knew his love for her was gone. He was going to utter some sort of protestation, but she stopped him, and said her woman's intuition told her he loved Fanny Morgan; let him marry her by all means, and may God bless them both. It was the general opinion that Susanna Dash's heart was broken, though the fracture took a long time accomplishing. We spinsters know more about these things than you give us credit for.'

"Did Aunt Rachel mean to hint that she had a love story locked up in her lacerated bosom too? If so, the annuity must have counteracted the heartbreaking in a marvellous manner, indeed.

"The marriage was not a happy one. You will not expect me to say anything against my own mother; but I fancy she was a little extravagant, and looked upon my father's really large income as unlimited. We lived in grand style—at least our parents did—I can recollect that. As for myself and my brother Morris, who was a year older than myself, we saw little of my father, and almost nothing of my mother. She left us greatly to the tender mercies of the servants; and though they were kind enough, still it was not like being with our parents. I remember what we enjoyed most of all was having a romp with my father when my mother went out by herself. But she seldom did this. She made him dance attendance upon her much against his will; and when they were both at home, she did not like us to be with them. She was very fond of him, and I think felt jealous of his partiality for us.'

" 'A mother jealous of her own children,' I moralized. 'Surely that is impossible.'

" 'I've been told not, my dear, by those who know. You may find it out one of these days.'

" 'I pray God, never, aunt!'

" 'Well, Amen. I was only five years old when something happened. I don't know what it was, but I can guess, and so can you. We never saw my mother any more. There was no trial or exposé, or anything of that kind. People were not so fond of washing their soiled linen in public then as they seem to be now. My father and mother separated quietly, and we all left Mudwalla, never to return. We migrated to Zoar, where my father invested his capital in the business your worthy relatives have just disposed of so summarily, and died at a good old age, leaving it to Morris, without taking any thought of me. It seemed to be settled beforehand that I was to be an old maid, my dear, and therefore (so they argued), needed no taking care of; whereas surely in my capacity of unprotected female I stood especially in need of care.'

" 'Of course,' I said, by way of propitiating the old dame.

" 'Yes, everybody is ready enough to say "of course," only nobody acts up to their principles in that respect. No, it's tacitly agreed upon that spinsters are a superfluous element in society, and must not be encouraged.'

" 'There's only one remedy,' suggested Alec.

" 'What's that?' asked my aunt.

" 'Polygamy,' he answered.

" ' Polly who?' My aunt was innocent of long words.

" ' Polygamy—letting a man have as many wives as he likes and can support.'

" ' Be quiet,' said my aunt, pretending to be greatly scandalized at the notion.

" ' See how nicely it would have settled all difficulties in the case of Fanny Morgan and Susanna Dash.'

" ' Or Percy, Mr. Moddle, and yourself,' replied my aunt, in a splendid Tu quoque. ' Be just to the sexes, if we are going to alter the marriage laws.'

" ' By all means. Only your sex is so largely in excess, that such a remedy would only increase the disease.'

" ' Well, then, to jump on to another generation,' continued this female Nestor, ' my brother Morris—your grandfather, Elsie—did as his father had done before him, married, and had a family—William, Edward, Sam, and poor Phillis. Susanna Dash, who long outlived Lloyd, came to Zoar, and bought the Topaz Farm, so as to be near Morris, to whom she had taken a great liking for his dead father's sake. She lived to be able to discriminate between the brothers so far that she liked William for his likeness to his father and grandfather. Edward she was the means of bringing up to the law, for she discerned in him quali- ties which she could not admire, but which she felt would get him on in the world. Sam she abominated, calling him a sniveller and a hypocrite; and eventually she quitted the world, leaving behind her a will which bore a lie on the face of it, or else proved her to have been insane when she made it —that is the will which was propounded by Llewellyn and Son——'

" 'But which is not the will at Doctors' Commons,' said Alec, feeling his turn had come to say something.

" 'And pray how do you know that, Mr. Wiseacre?' asked my aunt, looking im- mensely pleased—for his intelligence squared with her preconceived ideas.

" 'Only from having seen it, that's all,'

replied Alec. 'A shilling at Doctors' Commons procures you the sight of any testamentary document in which you feel interest.'

" 'Do you mean to tell me that you have seen Susanna Dash's will at Doctors' Commons, and that it does not square with what Edward Llewellyn represented it to be ?'

" 'That I cannot tell you, because I do not find that Edward Llewellyn has proved any will at all. He seems to have divided the property according to his *own* will and pleasure.'

" 'And yet you have seen the will of Susanna Dash, leaving it to Morris ?'

" 'Until William came of age, yes. What then ?'

" 'Well, then, all I can say is, you are a pair of fools.' Miss Rachel Llewellyn rather prided herself on being brusque on occasions.

" 'We rise to acknowledge the compliment, aunt, or would do so only it would look formal; but what would you have us do?'

" 'Threaten Edward Llewellyn with legal proceedings; and do so at once—before I die!'

" 'Have you any intention of departing within the next quarter of an hour?' I asked.

" 'Don't talk nonsense. Listen to what I have got to say. Put it to Sheppard in as lucid a form as you can, and consult him as to whether you should not commence proceedings at once.'

" 'We now reach,' said my Aunt Rachel, assuming quite the air of a regular narrator, 'a period after the death of Susanna Dash, when the " boys," as they were still termed, had grown up to be men, and were very much what you find them now. Your father, Elsie, was—well he was exactly what you can see him at present—a good-natured fool, if you will pardon my saying so, that the first sharper can impose upon him who thinks it worth his while to do so.

11—2

Your uncles, having cheated him out of
marbles and toffee in childhood, and appropriated all his pocket-money in more
advanced youth, set themselves deliberately
to the work of fleecing him in early man-
hood. Morris had put William into the
business—these two young gentlemen,
Edward and Sam, being much too genteel
to soil their hands with the yard measure.
Besides, they argued, and rightly enough,
shop-keeping "don't pay" as it used to.
Small profits and quick returns had got to
be the order of the day instead of long
credit and high prices. So Edward got
articled to a heavy lawyer, and looked
about for a wife with money. Sam found
piety and money-lending the most lucrative
combination that came to hand. Their
method of pilling their brother was to get
over their father.'

"'But Mr. Morris Llewellyn was in
possession of all his faculties, was he not?'
inquired Alec.

"'Well, my dear,' she replied, 'there was

a period in the history of all the male
Llewellyns—I say nothing of the women-
folk—at which I think it would have been
extremely rash for any to hazard the
assertion that they were, as you so pertinently term it, in full possession of their
faculties. My father had the family failing
when he behaved as he did to Susanna
Dash, and afterwards shut his eyes until it
was too late to my mother's delinquencies.
You have seen William suffer so badly from
this disease that he got shut up in a mad-
house, and Morris was very near running
the same risk. He shaved the edges of
the lunatic asylum by behaving like a
lunatic at home, and doing just what his
two unscrupulous sons told him.'

" ' And that was——'

" ' Well, first and foremost to draw up
that iniquitous will leaving Topaz equally
divided among his family, instead of letting
it go as Susanna Dash intended it, to
William only.'

" ' But how do you know this ?'

"'On Morris's own testimony. After he had done the deed he became very low and desponding; indeed he was mad then, and mad up to the time of his death, whatever he had been before. He called me to him one day when the young gentlemen were off guard for a moment, and after making all sorts of mops and mows, just as William holds his head when he has the family failing on him, he said, "Oh, Rachel, I've wronged you and William; but mind, after I'm dead, don't think hardly of me; the boys made me do it." "Made you do what?" I asked; but before he could answer Edward and Sam came in, and I could get no more then. He used to be always mumbling about "the annuity, the annuity—Rachel's annuity," which I pretty well understood, so far, that is, as I can be said to understand it now; but Edward and Sam either bullied the poor old man into silence, or else explained it by saying that, in his efforts to do me justice, he had burdened his estate with an annuity which he feared would deprive his children of their rights. "But we've told him we're ready to make the sacrifice, aunt," added Sam, who generally did the lying part of the business, leaving the legal portion to Edward. I used to call Edward the Law and Sam the Gospel, with every apology for using the words in such connexion.'

"'But then about Aunt Phillis?'

"'There, I wish I could hold my tongue, but I can't, though poor Phillis is dead and gone. She knew it all, and was a party to it all, I'm afraid ; but I make excuses for her. Those boys were too much for her and her poor weak old father. Some slender remains of decent brotherly feeling, it would seem, made them include her among the Topaz inheritors, and otherwise provide for her pretty fairly—very differently from what they did for me. It might have been brotherly feeling, or it might have been that she was obliged to be made a party to the transaction, and demanded high terms for connivance. She had, as you know, a cold, clammy sense of duty, and would not swerve except under strong temptation.'

"'And you think money and lands formed such a temptation?' I asked.

"'I'm afraid so.'

"'So then you really mean to tell me,' Alec went on, 'that Llewellyn and Son—for Percy, I take it, now comes on the tapis—were venturesome enough to draw up that will for Morris Llewellyn, and deposit it in Doctors' Commons, side by side with a document that gave the lie to its every clause?'

"'When Susanna's will was put there, Edward and Sam were young at their business, or perhaps they were obliged to prove some will of Susanna Dash's, and hadn't time to concoct a fresh one; for she died suddenly and took most of us by surprise. Percy was then articled to his father, and you a long-legged hoyden of a girl, Elsie——'

"'Still harping on my legs!'

"'So the best plan they could hit upon was to find out that you were made for one another, since a marriage between you would obviate the necessity of those two rather contradictory doucuments ever being disturbed.'

" ' But the Welsh estates—the Mudwalla property? According to what you say, Topaz must have been valueless in comparison of these,' urged Alec.

" ' Quite so; and about these I own myself in the dark. Many of Morris's words and looks, before he died in a weak-minded kind of way too, led me to think that he had done something bigger than the Topaz business—something especially that touched me—and that would be the case if he made ducks and drakes of his own and Susanna's Welsh possessions. My father's own property might have been all invested in the Zoar business. I think it was; but Susanna's property is as completely lost as the Ten Tribes of Israel.'

" ' We have recently been told that those lost Tribes are identical with the English nation,' said Alec. ' I don't know how far the theory will hold water; but I will move heaven and earth to discover that lost property. If that lawyer and money-lender have appropriated Topaz, depend upon it they have not neglected their larger interests in Wales.'

" ' Trust them,' said my aunt.

" ' If you could only give me the slightest clue to the whereabouts, I would run down and see who was in possession—to whom the rents were paid——'

" ' And get brought back again in custody of the police on a charge of wilful murder,' said my aunt.

" ' Such a fatality is not going to attach to every expedition I make,' replied Alec; ' but I am helpless. I don't know where to go. I couldn't go to the station and ask the booking-clerk for a ticket to Mudwalla, or my Welsh estates.'

" ' Sam and Edward would put you in a lunatic asylum if you did.'

" ' I have no doubt they would very much like to get me inside the walls of one of those establishments,' said Alec. 'It's astonishing what facilities such institutions afford to unscrupulous lawyers, who wish to modify family arrangements.'

" 'What do you mean to do, Alec,' I asked, ' in reference to these very important disclosures made by Aunt Rachel ?'

" ' Wait,' he said.

" ' Wait,' she continued, ' until I can say no more; in other words until I'm dead, which in the ordinary course of things can't be long, and then commence the case without even the depositions of one of the most important witnesses being taken ?'

" I think my aunt expected Alec would fetch a magistrate there and then, and get her to make an affidavit. The one wish of her life at present was to make an affidavit about something, and so put a spoke in the wheel which was hurrying the younger branches of the family to destruction.

" 'He's got the family failing like the rest,' she exclaimed. 'If Sam could only catch him now, he would make him sign away all

his wife's rights as easily as possible. Go
and bury your beak in the sand like the
ostrich, and fancy it's all serene because you
see nothing.'

" With this elegant ornithological simile,
Aunt Rachel concluded her revelations for
the time being, declining to add another
word until we had partaken of something
nice and hot for supper. She was a
gourmand in her way, and made it her
boast that she did not know the taste of
pure water.

" ' Mrs. Baker brought the savoury meat
to my aunt's bedside, where we all partook
of it in Bohemian fashion. She certainly
is the limpest, and most washed-out looking
widow I ever saw. Since her daughter's
death she seems to have resigned herself to
circumstances, and to have lost everything
in the shape of energy and effort. She
looked quite scared at Alec, as though
she expected he would hold her responsible for the troubles he had undergone
through her daughter, and perhaps bring

an action against her for false imprison-
ment.

"'Mrs. Baker,' he said, 'I feel you and I
ought to know one another. We should
have known each other long since, had
things not taken the terrible turn they did ;
for I was quite determined, had your poor
daughter not confided to you what she did
to me, that I would do so. It was a secret
I could not bear to have in my keeping,
and either Mrs. Lund or myself would have
spoken to you on the subject.'

"'No, sir, but did Mary really confess to
you about Mr. Percy?'

"'Mr. Percy Llewellyn, I suppose, per-
suaded you that this was only an ingenious
method of defence he adopted, to shift the
onus from myself to him.'

"'That was what he said, sir, and spoke
quite nicely about it too. He said you
were on trial for your life, and in such a
position, a man was bound to do the best
for himself; "but," he added, "of course you
don't believe it, Mrs. Baker?"'"

"'And you didn't?'

"'Frankly, sir, I *did* not.'

"'Do you now?'

"'I am bound to.'

"'But apart from the verdict of the jury, have you a suspicion that I laid hands on Mary?'

"'Not the least.'

"'Would you mind telling me whether you think Percy is guilty?'

"'I feel sure of it.'

"'You do!' I said.

"'I *am* sure of it.'

"'At last the woman has come round to common sense,' added my aunt. 'How many times have I warned you to beware of that hypocritical parson, Mrs. Baker? Did I not give you my reason for not sitting under him, when I would tell no one else—not even Elsie, who was going to be married to him?'

"'You did, Miss Rachel. Oh, how I wish I had listened to you and poor Miss Phillis before it was too late!'

"'When everybody was wagging their tongues against my relative here, Mr. Lund, and even Phillis and I did the same on account of his following Elsie about, did we not tell you then, that Percy had another and a worse motive for being jealous of Mr. Lund, than the fact of his stealing away his lady-love, which was only natural and proper?'

"'Thank you,' said Alec.

"'You warned me over and over again, Miss Rachel; and when I think, how, with my eyes open, I neglected to do what a mother should have, I feel the poor darling's death at my door.'

"'But,' continued Alec, 'you say now you are sure Percy did this terrible deed. Have you any reason beyond the finding of the jury, and, I think I may add, the pretty general consent of Zoar, for believing me innocent and Percy guilty?'

"'I have, sir,' answered Mrs. Baker, hesitating.

"'Would you mind telling me what it is?'

"'You will think me superstitious.'

"'Never mind if I do; but I do not think it likely I shall. What is your reason?'

"'Do you know those lines about the "curse in a dead man's eye?"' she asked.

"'Bless the woman!' my aunt whispered to me, 'she makes one's flesh creep.'

"'I know the lines well, though I cannot for the moment remember where they occur;' and he quoted them in a solemn voice :—

> "'An orphan's curse would drag to hell
>   A spirit from on high;
>   But, oh! more terrible than that
>   Is the *Curse in a Dead Man's Eye!*'

"'When my poor dear girl's body was brought home, the morning she was found in the Fishponds,' proceeded Mrs. Baker, while we listened open-mouthed, 'Mr. Moddle and Mr. Percy, who had been most active in the search all night, followed, you may remember, into the shop.'

"'I saw them,' said I, 'and asked myself

Is it possible Percy could have done the deed?'

" 'It quite threw me off my guard; indeed, I had not the shadow of suspicion then; though, as Miss Rachel says, she and Miss Phillis had so often warned me; but when the dear child was carried upstairs and laid on her little bed, I went in with the two gentlemen to see her. Her eyes were closed when we came in, and some one was wiping the dirt and slime from her face, and wringing out her beautiful golden hair—see, here is a curl of it I always carry in my locket. As we stood at the bottom of the bed, my poor girl's eyes slowly opened wide, and really for one moment a hope shot across me that I had not lost her after all; but the bystanders closed them again, and Mr. Percy himself put two coins on to keep them shut. Do you know the silly fancy that shot through my mind when the poor eyes opened so strangely?'

" 'What?'

" 'That they looked reproachfully at Mr.

Percy, as if to say, "You who are now tending my body, brought me to my death." Of course it was only fancy; but the conviction came into my mind then, and has never left me since.'

" 'I have often wondered why it is,' said Alec, 'that photography is not pressed into the service of the law. No doubt upon the sensitive retina of the human eye, is fixed a picture of the last objects that formed the surroundings of the dead; and if, before time had elapsed for that picture to fade, it were developed as we develop the negative from a photograph, the form of the murderer would be plainly visible in the case of a violent death.'

" 'What a terrible illustration that would be of the line "The curse in a dead man's eye!" ' I could not help observing.

" 'If that development could have taken place, the last form that rested upon my poor girl's vision was, I now feel sure, Mr. Percy Llewellyn's.'

" 'I congratulate you upon your return

to your right mind at last,' said my aunt; 'and now, of course, with the usual consistency that seems to characterize us Zoar people, you will put every obstacle you can in the way of the police tracking out the offender and bringing him to justice.'

" 'I shall simply sit still,' the widow replied. 'I could do nothing for or against the ends of justice if I tried. I shall not try.'

" 'Recollect,' said Alec, very calmly but firmly, 'Mrs. Baker. that until the crime is really traced home to somebody people may still suspect me. The innocent suffer when the guilty escape. That is a very venerable proverb. The chain of evidence was indeed strong against me. I tremble when I think of the narrowness of my escape now. Some people may think the verdict was against the weight of evidence; and as long as that may be so, I shall go about with a possible stigma attaching to me.'

" 'Well,' said my Aunt Rachel, who was evidently longing for a drop of something comfortable, 'I think we have had enough of horrors for one while. Will you kindly bring me up some warm water, and we will have a glass of something to keep your excellent chops and tomato-sauce quiet, before we part. I have told such a long story myself to-night, that I cannot listen much longer to anybody.'

"It was still early when we left my aunt's, and we took a stroll in the quiet wintry night, up and down the cathedral green, speculating on the probabilities of the good old soul having nightmare after her hearty supper and subsequent potations.

"When Alec gets under the shadow of the old cathedral, either solus or with his second self, as he now calls me, he is pretty certain to grow didactic, and I know I shall not bore you if I jot down a word or two the 'big lad' said on this occasion. The west front of Zoar Cathedral is peculiarly rich in sculptured forms of the old Saxon kings and the saints of every age. I know no finer sight than the moonlight shimmering upon these relics of the auld lang syne, and on the night of which I write the scene seemed more than usually picturesque.

"'Why should it be, I wonder,' Alec suggested, 'that the sight of those old fellows up there, sitting shivering, as it seems, in the cold, uncompromising moonlight, should make one feel so correspondingly calm? I really do experience the sensation of what your satirical old aunt at one time calls the "family failing," at another the "Zoar peculiarity," coming over me. I mean I feel inclined to pack up our traps and be off to some unromantic suburban cottage near town, and there, cloistered with you and the old folks in our *rus in urbe*, forget Topaz and the business, and, above all, the Welsh estates. Verily, I believe these to be a mere Utopia, the latitude and longitude of which will never be fixed. Somebody is enjoying Susanna Dash's worldly goods: does it matter much more to us than it does to Susanna Dash herself, or one of those old, bowlegged, bearded gentlemen up there, who that somebody is?'

" 'Decidedly the Zoar air is affecting your mental constitution.'

" 'What shall we accomplish if we stir in the matter? We shall incur heavy expense, dreadful anxiety, and very possibly get no good by it all. We can *live* without all this. What do we want more? If we could only put it to one of those whose effigies are done in stone up there, and with whom "the fever called living is over at last"—indeed, has been for several centuries —I feel sure that would be the safe advice we should receive : "Dinna fash. Rest and be thankful." '

" 'And yet,' I added, ' how closely to the confines of the other world anxiety about the affairs of this one follows us! That old lady we have left was as anxious about the bows in her company cap, and the graceful fall of her state dressing-gown, ay, and as desirous to augment her poor annuity, as though she had another half century clear before her, whereas the time must necessarily be very short.'

" 'And what a supper the old lady ate and drank ! It really gives me prospective nightmare even to think over what she consumed. How truly such people seem to be among those whose sole end and aim in existence one feels inclined to set down as *fruges consumere.* Yes, we legislate for ourselves as though we were certain of immortality. Perhaps it is wisely ordained that we should do so. We should accomplish nothing if we knew how literally we were walking about with our lives in our hands.'

" Do you believe in coincidences, my dear Mrs. Fane? let me ask you in conclusion, as the clergymen say. To me the word seems rather a heathen one. There must have been, I think, something more than the mere memory of those chops and tomato-sauce, and that copious libation of cognac, to make our thoughts thus revert to the poor old lady whose hospitality we had been sharing. She must have been dying at the very time we spoke. She had divested herself of the company cap and state robe, and Mrs. Baker saw her comfortably settled for the night. In the morning the little servant went to her bedside, and found that she was not only settled for the night, but settled for ever, as far as this mundane sphere was concerned. She must have died directly Mrs. Baker left her, for she was quite cold and stiff when they found her in the morning.

"But there was another coincidence stranger even than the circumstance of our talking about her on the cathedral green at the very time when she must have been dying. By the morning's post there came a letter which lay unopened by her bedside when Alec and my father went in at Mrs. Baker's summons. The epistle was an official one from Edward Llewellyn, and when my father broke the seal, he found its purport to be that, in consideration of certain losses connected with the estate of the late Morris Llewellyn, Miss Rachel Llewellyn must be prepared for inevitable reduction in the amount of the annuity now receivable by her, if not (which was more probable) for its entire withdrawal, as the fund available for it had well nigh ceased to exist.

"The old lady had sagaciously anticipated the diminution of her already slender income, and soared to a sphere where annuities are unknown!"

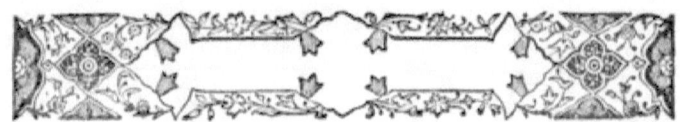

CHAPTER V.

THE RITUALISTIC SCARE.

ELOVED BRIGGS,—At last the *rus in urbe* is realized; and from the serene recesses of my suburban retreat I send this greeting to your still more sequestered abode in the little cathedral city.

"First let me congratulate you on the ecclesiastical intelligence contained in your letter. I am very glad you are put in to keep St. Simon Magus warm, as the phrase goes, because I have no doubt that is only the first step towards your being promoted to the incumbency; and do you know, Briggs, I don't think that singing a double daily service is enough to keep a man up to the mark. I have often suspected you of vegetating; but now you will have something to keep your animal and intellectual faculties employed.

"I wonder what is the meaning of Edward Llewellyn selling his presentations to St. Simon Magus. The Dean's object in buying that piece of preferment I can, as I have said, easily divine. You are a pre-destined incumbent, as well as a dignitary in Zoar. Really, Briggs, you are a very fortunate man.

"As for ourselves, Elsie has got back to her teaching, and I to my journalism again, just as though nothing had ever happened to break the even tenor of our way. We have exchanged our pretty little apartment for a house in the western suburbs, but I still retain one room in the old set for writing purposes. Unfortunately, I am very prone to be led astray from the paths of literature by the slightest distraction, and my foes are those of my own household. I dissipate in my wife's society, and run into all sorts of extravagant idleness with Mr. William Llewellyn who, having nothing to do himself, makes it his mission to prevent my doing anything too. Mrs. Llewellyn is always busy, about what, goodness knows; but her hands are never still. With one small servant she transacts all the business of our household; and, though she says never a word, she frowns us all into being industrious, when she sees us disposed to do the dolce far niente, and we are all of us a little inclined in that direction, I am afraid.

"Really when, from my present coign of vantage, I look back upon recent events in Zoar, I can scarcely persuade myself that they were real. It seems like a distempered dream; seems as though my good mother-in-law must always have been acting house-keeper here, and her husband setting himself to impede the frantic efforts of myself and wife to be industrious. I almost think I am beginning to congratulate myself on 'the law's delay' which keeps Sheppard shilly-shallying about our interests at Topaz and in Wales, and also—for I suppose all arises from the same source—prevents Percy from being caught, and brought to book for his crime. Every now and again, as you will have seen, the newspapers have mysterious paragraphs, saying that the police are now in possession of a clue to the Zoar mystery. For some of these I confess myself answerable, as I think it is best to keep public curiosity alive, and not let the 'mystery' sink too soon, as it seems destined to do, into the comprehensive category of undetected crimes. Others are, as far as I know, genuine, unless they emanate from some other imaginative writer who has as much foundation as myself for his assertion.

"'How it shakes one's faith in newspapers,' said Elsie, the other day, 'to be behind the scenes as I am.'

"'Yes,' I replied, 'I remember, in my days of innocence, I thought a leading article as trustworthy as a sermon.'

"'Your estimate of the two species of composition seems to have varied inversely of late.'

"'I wish you wouldn't talk shop,' was my rejoinder; 'you are an embodied Walkingame since you undertook the education of that pretty little Amy.'

"'Impudence!'

"Talking of those same sermons, though, Briggs, it is remarkable to what a conscientious extent I am fulfilling the promise made in my name at my baptism, that I should 'hear sermons.' If I were in Zoar, I should no doubt be one of your most persistent followers, and spot you on the instant if you ever dared to use an old MS. Mrs. Fane 'brought me round' as the phrase goes; for when I was a Zoar student, I scandalized everybody by my habitual neglect of religious ordinances. I thought I had found out a more excellent way. I fell into the mistake so many young men make who are ignorant of their own mental dimensions. I thought I had ultimated the knowable, and that positive science could be the guide of our footsteps in spiritual as well as other matters. Calling myself

Broad Church, I was simply theistic, and really wonder I did not break those bounds too, and sail away into blank atheism. I used to like nothing better, as you will remember, than offending you with my loose talk about faith and morals. It was *all* talk—all mere bombast and braggadocio, as is that of half your soi-disant sceptics. It's the fashion just now, or was in my student days, to have religious difficulties, just as it is to be short-sighted, and have to stick a glass in your eye. Thank goodness I fell into the hands of those two sensible women, my wife and Mrs. Fane. I cannot fail to discover something providential in the order of my acquaintance with them. Had I met with Mrs. Fane first, I should have set her down as simply churchy; but Elsie converted me with her strong common sense from my frigid materialism, and then Mrs. Fane took up the work where my wife left it (for she *was* my wife before the process was complete), and added the positive element of Anglicanism—I use the word technically and advisedly — to the previous negative condition of mere religionism.

"I shall not bore you with all this detail, I know; because I am sure my erratic course in bygone days was a real trouble to you.

"I hope I am, and believe I always was, a religious man; but I have only recently discovered how childishly impressionable I am to the external ordinances of religion. I have often felt very like a girl, in the facility with which a pathetic story or a beautiful strain of music brought tears to my eyes. It has also struck me as curious that I should take so acute a pleasure in seeing buds gem the trees in spring, or be so depressed when they fall sere and yellow from the branches in autumntide. I had no utilitarian interest in the leaves! And now something of the same kind occurs to me in ecclesiastical matters. The exquisite adaptation of the Church's provisions to man's requirements has been brought home to me. The first time I prayed—if I may touch on matters so private—was simply as a bold experiment. *That experiment succeeded;* and the isolated act deepened into a habit. Then came the other means of grace. The sacramental system displayed itself as the perfection of Heaven's response to earth's necessities. To me, it is such a privilege to unburden all those doubts and difficulties as they occur, that I avail myself fully of the ordinance of auricular confession, to which Mrs. Fane first attracted my notice. I wonder whether you will laugh at this, Briggs, and say, as even Elsie does, that it is just like my impetuosity to shoot off into the very opposite extreme to that from which I started. This seems to me normal enough. When once my previous condition of *un*-belief was done away, mere stagnation via media principles could not fill up the void. I must be as energetic on the positive as aforetime I was on the negative side. Hence it is that my condition of scepticism having been more advanced than Elsie's, so is my present position in the graduated scale of ecclesiasticism; but she is coming on very nicely. Listen to her—

" 'And so, Alec,' she asked me, 'do I understand that you seriously mean to assume the cowl?'

" 'As a lay brother of the third order yes, Elsie. Have you any objection?'

" 'None; except——'

" 'Except what?'

" 'I want you to be quite sure that your new fervour is not carrying you further than you will one day like.'

" 'Do you mean than I shall find expedient? Is it the medio *tutissimus* ibis you allude to?'

" 'Not in the least. I am thankful to say we have neither of us any inducements to trifle with our convictions in this way. Only *do* you really feel the ground steady under your feet? I don't know why I should ask you; but it is very nice to be able to do so without fear of wounding you or giving you offence.'

" ' And delightful, again, to know one's wife feels sufficient interest in one's spiritual condition to plead guilty to such an anxiety. I fancy most married people proscribe these subjects, as if to touch on them were a species of indelicacy.'

" ' Such a foolish diffidence does, I know, exist; and I am only too thankful we are unconscious of it. You are not like other men in this respect, Alec dear. The generality are very thick-skinned to all religious influences.'

" ' You are speaking from a Cousin Percy point of view. I don't believe my sex are so pachydermatous as you make them out.'

" ' I should very much like to see the interior of this Anglican monastery of which you tell me.'

" ' That you can't very well do; but we'll ask Pugin, the provost, to dinner one day. He is a fine specimen of the monks of old— or rather of the adaptation of the monastic

13—2

principle to the needs of the nineteenth century.'

" 'That is what I cannot understand. To me it seems an anachronism.'

" 'So it did to me once—an anachronism of the most glaring kind; but if you could only be present in that bijou chapel with its congregation of brethren in their quaint habits, and hear the Anglican Benediction Office succeed Compline, as the Litany of the Sacrament was chanted amid fumes of incense, and the Host elevated to the sound of silver bells, you would say, as I said, that it was the perfection of worship—the very crown and culmination of earthly existence.'

" 'Pugin has indeed converted you.'

" 'No, dear wife, that work was yours.'

" 'Well, he has put the coup de grâce to what I began, then.'

" 'Perhaps so.'

" Pugin is a wealthy clergyman who relinquished a valuable benefice in the country to come to London and establish a

Religious House in the suburbs for young
men engaged in business or study in town.
A few of the brethren only lead a strictly
religious life, residing altogether in the
monastery and keeping the 'seven hours'
diligently in chapel. The rest go, as I
said, to business during the day, but all
attend mass in the morning and Compline
at bedtime. Can you imagine anything
more likely to guard a young man against
the temptations of town than such a life as
this? They have a fine building close by
where we are living, and with their
refectory, library, and common-room, they
are as merry as the actual monks of old.
There is nothing ascetic in the arrangement
of the place, but everything is done by rule,
and exactly appears to me to fulfil the ideal
of men living *in* the world without being
of the world—using the world without
abusing it. Married men are allowed to
become brethren of the third order, and so
to attend services when they please, and
live in community occasionally. My father-

in-law and myself have both availed ourselves of this privilege.

"Staggered by the evil example of Mr.
Moddle, rather than dissatisfied with anything in Irvingism itself, Mr. Llewellyn
has, for the time being, seceded from that
body, though we occasionally pay a visit
together to the splendid church in Gordon
Square. There is very much in the external cultus of the Catholic Apostolic
Church with which I sympathize, though,
at the same time, much too that I cannot
embrace.

" Mr. Llewellyn and myself are about the
most eclectic worshippers you could find in
London, I should think. We wander
about from church to chapel, and generally
find something good in most places. I
utilize my expeditions by writing descriptive articles about them, but I believe,
at bottom, my father-in-law is honestly in
search of a religion. Mrs. Llewellyn
quietly dropped down into the first church
she came to, and has stuck faithfully to it

ever since. Elsie and I go with Mrs. Fane and Amy, when I am not starring it with some new sect. I chiefly attend the Monastery services on week days.

" I brought about the meeting between Elsie and Pugin. That led to an introduction to Mrs. Fane, and she immediately struck up a warm friendship with the Provost.

"' I like him,' she said to me. 'He is my ideal of a Churchman of the day; a perfect gentleman, yet a devoted servant of the Church. We want more such men, if we are to soar above the dead level of Establishmentarianism.'

"' What a nice long comforting word, mamma,' said little Amy, who was present.

"' Very much of the Mesopotamian order, Amy,' remarked Elsie.

"I have a very strong idea that Mrs. Fane, Elsie, and Amy were in the organ-loft of the choir chapel the last evening I was there, just for the sake of seeing me and Mr. Llewellyn in our Augustinian habits. Pugin would not like to do such a thing publicly, for fear of causing a scandal; but he would not mind smuggling a lady or two in just to gratify their curiosity; and I know they have been there from the way they tease my father-in-law and myself about the masonic secresy we think attaches to our monasticism.

"Of course this movement is derided on the one hand, and suspected on the other by those who know nothing about it, and will not take the trouble to inquire. As for Pugin himself, I consider him the *safest* man I know. The line he takes seems to me quite typical. He says, 'Why should I go to Rome? What can she offer me that I have not here already? I can understand a Low Churchman going over because he must sooner or later find an aching void in the merely negative system of Protestantism; but for an English Catholic to become a Romanist would be an unnecessary forfeiture of patriotism—nothing more or less. He would gain nothing in way of faith or practice, and simply put himself under foreign instead of national supremacy.

"You see, Briggs, on what a lofty and independent pinnacle the possession of the sevenfold sacramental system, with its necessary deductions, places us.

"But when I say this, do not, please, fancy that all is couleur de rose; far from it. If women—by which I do not mean only those of the female sex—would be logical, then our position would be secure; but almost all the women (I *do* mean females now) and a large portion of the third sex— as Sydney Smith calls the parsons—are the reverse of logical; and herein lies our danger. This has been the besetting weakness of the Tractarian movement from its first evolution down to its present development in Ritualism; it cannot reckon on its adherents. It ought to be a safeguard against Romanism. It is, on the contrary, the feeder of the Roman Church.

"We are—as you know slenderly from the

papers, but as I have reason to know more intimately—in the very thick of a Ritualistic scare. They come about in cycles and are perfectly epidemic when they do come. This promises to be a severe one.

"The most beautiful thing is to see how clear Pugin keeps of all these dangers. He is hand and glove with the Lowest of Low Churchmen, who cannot but be staggered at the earnest devotion of his young disciples. They are their best Sunday School teachers and lay helpers. They work missions, and never obtrude a single offensive doctrine. In a word, they answer so completely to the criterion ' By their fruits ye shall know them,' that Pugin is unmolested whilst everybody else is being attacked. Pugin has popular opinion to back him up, and the Bishops themselves cannot afford to brave that, even when badgering a Ritualist with a Public Worship Bill in hand.

"The consequence is that while the smaller men are persecuted and made martyrs of, Pugin goes on chanting his benedictions and making the oaken roof of the refectory ring with his jokes at the expense of the old ladies in lawn sleeves.

"'I can cross swords with an honest Broad Churchman,' he said, one day at dinner with Mrs. Fane, where we all formed a sort of religious family party. 'I don't like Evangelicals personally, but I know they are sincere. It's your five and ten thousand pounders I cannot get at. I sit and do reduction sums to see how much they make a day by their Platitudinarianism— another polysyllable for you, Amy—and I know I can't get at them anyhow, because I can't touch their State wages, and they are invulnerable everywhere else.'

"'But surely, Father Pugin, such Bishops as these are a blot on your State Church.'

"'Would you improve it by going to Rome? Are the annals of the Papacy clean?'

"'But Pius IX., dear old man, is above suspicion.'

"'Pius IX.—dear old man, I grant you—

is in the furnace of affliction. If England became Roman to-morrow, what guarantee have you that a Borgia might not fill the chair?'

"'Cardinal Manning would probably fill the chair before England would be Catholicized.'

"'Excuse me. England *is* Catholic.'

"'Romanized, then, if you like. Cardinal Manning is not a Borgia.'

"'Dear old man—I repeat your encomium—no. Nor is Monsignor Capel; but I don't think I should like to be a priest under either of them as well as under John of London or Archibald of Canterbury.'

"'Would you not, indeed?'

"'Certainly not.'

"Mrs. Fane looked in mild wonderment at her adored Padre, who administered a gentle reproof what time he munched his olive and sipped his claret.

"'You are, if you will pardon the remark, my dear friend, the most indiscreet person in the world, and will do infinite harm to the cause by thus displaying your proclivity towards Rome.'

"'What am I doing?' she asked, lifting up her white hands in assumed despair.

"'Well, first of all, like a good many others of our party, I confess, you haunt the Pro-cathedral and other Roman places of worship. Why you should do so I cannot imagine.'

"'It is so nice,' she exclaimed.

"'Delicious,' echoed little Amy.

"'That may be; though I cannot see in what respect the "Pro" is nicer or more delicious than All Saints, Margaret Street.'

"'No vestments.'

"'Or Father West's.'

"'Only white ones that look like Protestant surplices in a transition state.'

"'Supposing they were only Protestant surplices, not even undergoing that metamorphosis at all; you should be content to wait, and not compromise the cause by attending a foreign place of worship.'

" ' Foreign ! You surely confess the Roman to be a branch of the Catholic Church.'

" ' Of course I do; but still I say, to attend a Roman instead of an Anglican church, is to desert the national for a foreign place of worship; and just at this crisis you ought not to do it.'

" ' What is the crisis?' I asked; for Elsie and myself had been silently listening to this passage-at-arms between the two friends.

" ' I will tell you,' he said, ' in confidence, though I fear it will not be long before all will be known. There is a movement—a fairly influential one — abroad for the Ritualists to join the Roman Catholic Church, on condition of certain unimportant concessions being made to them.'

" ' Indeed,' said Mrs. Fane, with glistening eager eyes. ' Then the time is coming at last for which I have been so long desirous.'

" ' What time?'

"'For the reunion of a divided Christendom. It has been for years the one aspiration of my heart.'

"The way this remark was received by the different constituents of our eclectic dinner-party was very characteristic indeed.

"My mother-in-law said nothing. She had solved the problem of reunion for herself by making no sort of distinction between church and chapel, Roman, Anglican, or Nonconformist. Will the question ever be settled in any other way? That was what I thought; so I held my peace and spake nothing too. It is an attitude I am beginning greatly to assume in reference to these vexed questions about Church matters. We talk too much and do too little. A slight infusion of practical Christianity, like Mrs. Llewellyn's, would do more to pour oil on the waves than all your Eirenica and Tracts on Toleration.

"'The end won't be brought about in that direction,' said Father Pugin, dogmatically.

"My father-in-law smiled a sarcastic smile, and observed—

"'Directly such an event takes place the Dispensation will be over, the Millennial Period commence, and the Personal Reign begin.'

"Little Amy's remark was the most pertinent of all. She said—

"'What a number of different opinions you good people seem to have about these matters. Can't you agree?'

"'In the multitude of counsellors there is wisdom, Amy,' I said.

"'Too much wisdom for me.'

"Then Elsie broke silence, and assuming the schoolmistress, said—

"'I tell you what we will do, Amy, you and I, we will stand on the shore and watch the winds and waves at war——'

"'Have a care, Amy,' I said; 'she is giving you a Latin quotation in disguise, like a powder lurking in raspberry jam.'

"'Oh yes, Mrs. Lund, that is just what I like to do at Dover or Folkestone, and watch the people coming in by the Channel boats looking so delightfully ill.'

"'Yes,' rejoined Mrs. Fane, 'but we have now got a good ship *Castalia* that will carry us over the warring winds and waves. Seriously, Father Pugin, what attitude do you mean to take in reference to this movement?'

"'I am deeply interested in it.'

"'But cannot join it?'

"'No.'

"'I am at a loss to conceive why.'

"'I have told you, and I believe my course is a consistent and intelligible one. I demur to placing the English Church once more in Roman bondage.'

"'And rather than do that—rather than submit to the Holy Father—you would keep her an "Establishment" under the nominal headship of the Queen, the real supremacy of a heathen parliament.'

"'Your alternative is exaggerated, but even so, yes. I am content to labour and to wait.'

" 'I don't forget, Father Pugin, that you are my spiritual director,' answered Mrs. Fane, with much solemnity; 'but I tell you, and with you all these my dear friends, that my conscience points me in another direction. If the Old Catholic movement only opens a way for the fusion of the Anglican and Roman branches of the Catholic Church, I shall be one of the very first to throw myself into the arms of Rome.'

" ' If you are leaning on the Old Catholic movement, that is a broken reed indeed. Rome hates the Old Catholics even more cordially than those she nicknames Protestants.'

" ' Meaning Anglicans.'

" ' Yes; they are foes in her own household. No; you will have to submit unconditionally, and as Anglicans, to Roman supremacy, if at all.'

" ' Not unconditionally.'

" ' Depend upon it, yes.' And so the religious discussion broke up for the time being.

" Mrs. Fane manages to collect around her the most heterogeneous sets of people at her evening receptions. T. and P. at Gower Street could have been only the feeblest indication of these wonderful reunions. To pass by the mere bigwigs and leaders of fashion, whose names would not, I know, interest you, here you meet the recognised chiefs of all the religious parties in ecclesiastical London; and I amuse myself with jotting down the names of these in my notebook as so many chapters in a forthcoming work on the Faiths of the Metropolis, actually dividing them into High, Low, and Broad, and as-signing a volume apiece to them. But, be-sides these, Catholicism—I ought, of course, to say Roman Catholicism—puts in its appearance in the persons of its very highest dignitaries. You see a Jesuit priest elbowing an Evangelical parson, and a Puseyite in the seventh heaven of delight at being talked to as a man and a brother by Monsignor Capel, or the Cardinal himself, while the Broad Church ecclesiastics flit about from sectary to sectary as if proclaiming the glad tidings that the Millennium of Latitudinarianism had commenced. At the extreme North Pole a few of the upper-crust of Nonconformity, chiefly, I must confess, Unitarians, make up the motley group.

"On the evening succeeding the after-dinner conversation I have quoted, Father Pugin sat by Mrs. Fane's side complacently surveying all the varied groups, while she openly proclaimed—for she prides herself upon outspokenness—that the time had come for healing the breaches and fraterniz-ing with Rome.

"'So, all you good people,' she said, to the group immediately around her, 'just go to the Cardinal or Monsignor, or, failing these, to the first Roman priest you find, and make the best terms you can.'

"At these words the Unitarians and Broad Churchmen scowled or smiled. The Evangelicals—the few who were there—popped their crush-hats and fled; while the Ritua-

lists looked to Father Pugin as their fugle-
man, to see whether he would, like Lars
Porsena, lead the way to Rome.

"Father Pugin made no sign, however,
and the evening resolved itself into music,
and light conversation.

"But, in the meantime, the Ritualistic
scare, as the secular papers term it, is at its
height. Whether Mrs. Fane's words really
did fire the train already prepared or not,
of course, I cannot tell; but the train is
fired, and you cannot guess how much the
women have to do with this. Female poli-
ticians bring about all our great parliamentary changes. Command the Ladies'
Gallery and you are safe. Marriage with a
Deceased Wife's Sister will be carried if
you can once persuade the women to give
over calling it the "Sisters' Marriages"
Bill. But in religious, or rather in ecclesiastical matters, women are as clever as
Polish ladies in espionage. I am really
half disposed to credit this clever and
fascinating little Mayfair widow with

a considerable portion of our present fracas.

"There are, of course, other ladies at work, who are neither clever nor fascinating. I mean those episcopal old ladies the Bench of Bishops. Armed with their flagellum of the Public Worship Bill, these old harridans are doing their best to drive out of the Church of England all the zeal, scholarship, and culture she possesses. Whither they drive it matters not to them, as long as they rid themselves of all that disturbs their quieta non movere method. Rome smiles, and infidelity chuckles to see the way these idiotic Mrs. Partingtons trundle their mops to squeeze out the Atlantic, and sweep away all remnants of Catholicism with the besom of destruction. But I am forgetting that my Briggs is a mild dignitary himself on the high road to promotion. He may be destined to repose in the castellated episcopal palace of Zoar, cut off by moat and drawbridge from the outside world. But even Bishop Briggs, despite

his moat and portcullis, will have to be reminded sometimes that there is a world
elsewhere. I will not tread unnecessarily
on Briggs' proleptically episcopal corns, but
I must, Cassandra-like, put on record my
opinion that the present policy of the
bishops is suicidal.

"Ecce signum ; there is no longer any
doubt that a very considerable portion of
the Ritualistic body have approached the
highest representative of Roman Catholicism in England, and through him sounded
Pope Pius IX. as to the terms of surrender.
From my position as member of the staff of
a daily paper (such is now my proud position, Briggs), I am enabled to say that the
question of England as a temporary residence for the Sovereign Pontiff is being
gravely discussed. Fancy Mrs. Grundy
hearing the news that Pope Pius had dis-
embarked, carpet-bag in hand, from the
Castalia ! A counter coup has been got
up for the moment by the remonstrant
Ritualists, who, following the lead of Father

Pugin, are at present swayed by patriotism and held back by an esprit de corps which I thoroughly appreciate. But in the meantime Mrs. Partington is abroad with her mop and besom, and at any moment something may occur to change the minds of this very 'considerable minority.' One bishop bullies the Wesleyans, whose title to the appellation of 'Rev'd' is, I am beginning to think, as good as their lordships' own to that of 'Fathers in God.' Then another will have the devil dogmatically defined and made an article in the creed—which that exceedingly objectionable personage is not at present. In a word, the elements of chaos are upheaving, and the probable result looks symptomatic of anything but order; and I do not believe that it is the Divine Spirit which, through the rulers of the Church, causes the commotion.

"'I'm going down to the reading-room of the British Museum, Elsie,' I said, on the morrow of the discussion at dinner.

"'Don't overwork yourself, Alec. Journalism is enough for one man's brain. What are you going to read up now ?'

" 'The Nag's Head Controversy. I begin to doubt about the succession."

" Elsie put down her book or her work, I forget which it was, and looked at me so seriously, that I wondered what was the matter.

" 'I am going to make a proposal to you, Alec.'

" 'It isn't leap year. Besides, I proposed to you, and was accepted, a long while since. You haven't forgotten that we are very much married, have you ?'

" ' By no means.'

" ' What is the proposal then ?'

" 'That we simply—you and I—do not trouble ourselves with this religious question.'

" ' How so ?'

" ' Let us be philosophers.'

" ' What, drift back to unbelief ?'

" ' No ; I don't call that philosophy now, no more do you, thank God. That was only a passing affection—I might put in another syllable, and say affectation—incidental to our mental childhood. We have grown out of that.'

" 'And you think I have grown up at one bound into intellectual senility?'

" 'No, not exactly.'

" 'Something uncommonly like it, though.'

" 'I think you are swayed greatly by your feelings in this matter, and I believe the best thing for us—for you, as an impartial journalist, and for me as a teacher and a writer in my own small way—would be to keep our heads cool.'

" ' By all means; but look here, Elsie, if you felt that the present position of the religious question was such as to promote *ir*religion and sap morality, what would you do? What would you have me do?'

" ' For myself, I should stand aloof from the subject altogether. I should imitate my mother's example, and go to the quietest,

most old-fashioned church I could find at
hand, or even stay away altogether, if the
atmosphere of unrest penetrated even
thither. and then I would commune with
Heaven in the secresy of my closet.'

" ' But for me ?'

" ' Your mission would probably be to
write stinging leaders, according to your
conscience, of course, against those you
thought in the wrong; but I should
decidedly leave the subject at the office, as
you do political matters and sanitary
questions which you have to touch.'

" ' But I can't leave these behind as I
can the political. Sanitary questions can't
be disposed of so summarily as you think.
Even when I have written my article on
Asthenopolis I have to look to my own
drains, and bully the contractor until he
gets my dustbin emptied. So it is with
these ecclesiastical questions. They follow
me home and penetrate to the very core of
my common life.'

" ' Do they ?'

" ' Most certainly, yes. I cannot, now I have outgrown unbelief, realize what you call the philosophic condition of mind. It must be a matter of temperament, and the woman can entertain these things more calmly than the man.'

" ' Perhaps so. If so, all the better for the woman.'

" ' Then, in treating these subjects in leaders, one is never allowed to speak out. One has to praise the Public Worship Bill, or at least one must only be mildly satirical at the best. Bishops are to be treated respectfully, and the ideal of excellence is to be the National Church as at present constituted.'

" ' Have you ever ventured to ask where you will find a more satisfactory model? It is just as with our English climate; folks abuse it until they try another. Perspiring at the Tropics, or frozen up in the Arctic Regions, they long for the grey skies and fitful alternations of sunshine they growled about of old.'

" ' Humph !'

" ' You know they say it is a good, practically useful climate. There are more days on which you can go out with impunity than anywhere else, I believe. We have been very nearly frozen in Rationalism; don't let's frizzle in Romanism.'

" ' Mrs. Fane will.'

" ' That I cannot say—cannot help. I speak of ourselves.'

" ' You put it in the plural, as much as to say, if I went you would be sure to follow.'

" ' I should, of course, be greatly swayed by your conduct; and should dread above all else the shadow of division or disagreement in this matter.'

" Of course I don't tell Elsie that I think her right. When you are married, Briggs, and incumbent of St. Simon Magus, perhaps tenant at Topaz Farm, you will, at an early stage of your matrimonial career, learn the policy of not confessing that your wife gets the better of you in conjugal discussions.

Act on the conviction; but by no means formulate it in words.

"And yet I think she *is* right; and, as you are not a Benedict yet, I don't mind telling you so. I feel sure it would be better for me to keep my head cool, and not take sides in this controversy; but I can't accomplish this. It's a mercy I'm not a parson, for I should be a red-hot controversialist in the pulpit and parish, the very living embodiment of the odium theologicum. My peculiarity interferes with my newspaper work. I find they don't give me the religious leaders to write any longer, because they have to cancel so much of my matter, and I cannot get my remarks into less than three columns, instead of a column and a quarter; while they have stopped my descriptive articles too, for the avowed reason that they are no longer descriptive, but declamatory—so they say. I shall let the steam off by writing a religious novel, elevating all the Ritualists to the Episcopal Bench, and making all the

Evangelicals and Dissenters perish miserably. It would do me good.

" What would do me more good, old fellow, and what I shall really try to carry out, would be to run down to Zoar, to smoke quiet pipes with you, and hear you warble your melodious inflections in the dear old cathedral, which has so many pleasant associations for me. I could then prod Sheppard into something like activity in the Topaz matter and the High Street business. I could even run across the Bristol Channel and look after the Welsh estates. I am tired of paying money for Sheppard or his clerks to do this to no purpose. I feel sure that when they want a constitutional they take it in Wales, and put it down to my account.

" What do you think ? I had an adventure, or what might easily have been expanded into an adventure, last night.

" In the ordinary course of my office duties I have a good deal to do with the police. If a dreadful murder or anything of that kind is on the tapis, I am immediately laid under contribution. Perhaps the editor believes that I was, after all, the hero of the Zoar mystery, and so am qualified to appreciate a murder as what De Quincey called 'one of the fine arts.' I often discuss the Zoar business with the inspectors and men, and am amused with the pompous air they assume as they tell me the authorities are close on the heels of Percy Llewellyn, whom they have set down, without judge or jury intervening, as the undoubted doer of the deed. They assume that he is at the Antipodes at least, and must have expended a small fortune in hunting him by means of emissaries and telegrams to the uttermost ends of the earth. Percy, however, is still at large, though he has been a hundred times reported on the eve of being arrested.

"A night or two ago I was standing, during the small hours, at the door of the Bow Street station, talking to a police-sergeant, and waiting for a homeward-bound cabman open to a bargain. I was muffled to the eyes, for the early morning was cold, and I had been writing all the evening in a stuffy office with the gaslight beating down upon my head. I was on the point of hailing a hansom when a man passed by the station door, swathed in a long light-coloured Ulster coat with the collar up, so as to conceal his face to the same extent as my own was hidden. He seemed to lurch or make a movement towards me, just as if he meant to come into the station. I really almost stood aside to let him do so, and the sergeant, noticing my movement, did the same. I let the cab go hopelessly by, and for one instant my eyes met those of the stranger.

" It was no stranger. *It was Percy Llewellyn !*

" ' Did you know that man, sir ?' said the sergeant.

" I burdened my conscience by answering in the negative; for I was taken off my guard, and then so ashamed to confess it, that I did not like to say—

" ' Yes, give chase.'

" ' I believe he was going to give himself up for something or other if he hadn't seen you,' added the sergeant, with a laugh. ' What, going to walk after all ?'

" ' Yes ; good-night.'

" ' Good-night, sir. It was a pity you missed that cab.'

" ' I shall soon find another.'

" Not a minute elapsed between my seeing Percy at the door and starting in pursuit as fast as I could. I have no distinct idea what I meant to do, whether to call a policeman and give him in charge, or speak to him on my own account. All I am conscious of is a desire to overtake him, and I almost ran from the station to Long Acre, which was the direction he had taken. There was no sign of him. Could I have been mistaken ? It was impossible. I could swear to that bright, bead-like eye with its sinister glance. It rested for an instant on

me as if impelled by some strange fascination.
I might have believed the whole thing a
mere hallucination, if the sergeant had not
been with me and noticed the man's peculiar
lurch towards the station-house door. However, it was no use hunting. The street
was perfectly empty. I resolved to do what
I felt I ought to have done at the very
first, overcome my false shame and tell the
sergeant what I had seen. I went back to
the station.

"'What, thought better of the walk,
sir?'

"'Sergeant,' I said, disregarding his
question, 'do you know who that man was
that seemed inclined to come into the
station just now?'

"'No; do you?'

"'Yes; it's Percy Llewellyn.'

"'The man we want for the Zoar
murder?'

"'The same—my cousin.'

"The officer gave a loud merry laugh,
and looked at me, as much as to ask where

15—2

I had been refreshing, or whether I had gone clean off my head.

"'No, no, sir. He's far enough from London; and, if he wasn't, depend upon it one of the last places he would be found at, would be the door of Bow Street Police-station. They generally give us a pretty wide berth.'

"'But men have given themselves up for murders before now; and you saw he was half inclined to come in. Perhaps, as you said, I did scare him away.'

"'If he wanted to give himself up, there was a double opportunity for him, which might never occur again. No; the people who give themselves up generally turn out in the morning to have taken a drop too much;' and again the officer looked at me as if to satisfy himself whether this favourite explanation would not meet my case.

"'You can act upon it or not, sergeant, as you will,' I rejoined. 'I am not sure I wish the wretched man to be arrested;

but if my life depended on it, I could swear that was Percy Llewellyn. Good-night, once more.'

" ' Good-night, sir, again.'

" I got a cab before I left the street, and had the curiosity to crane my neck out of the window, so as to ascertain whether the sergeant did or did not act on my information. Quite a little file of men came out of the station, and dispersed in different directions, according to his instructions. It was only official reserve, and the fact of his having broached the theory of Percy being at the Antipodes, which prevented his acting avowedly on my 'tip.' If he succeeded, he would expect me to write a long congratulatory paragraph on the activity and intelligence of the metropolitan police, in arresting this notorious 'suspect,' without any sort of clue to his whereabouts, and when all evidences pointed to his being secreted in some distant hiding-place.

" I told nobody but Elsie what I had seen. She impertinently asked me where I had supped; but finding that I was really serious, she said—

" ‘I am glad you acted as you did. Perhaps the hesitation was providential. Should we, or would the poor dead girl, be any better off if Percy were brought to justice, and all the terrible story raked up again?’

" ‘Not a bit.’

"So, like thorough optimists, we settled that things were best as they are. I think I would not mention this occurrence, Briggs; or, at all events, not to anybody but the Dean—to whom give our kindest remembrances; but I am as clearly conscious as I am of my own existence, that my eyes have rested on Percy Llewellyn, and that he is not — or was not — in any distant retreat, but here, lost in London."

CHAPTER VI.

THE INTRIGUE WITH ROME.

EAR MR. BRIGGS,—See the perils of your influential position as officiating minister at St. Simon Magus, Zoar. Alec says I am to call you a warming-pan, but I cannot bring myself to do that. We all fly to you in our troubles and difficulties; and if the Zoar ladies are at all like what they used to be when I pestered my present husband into marrying me, they will have a good many troubles and difficulties to lay before such an eligible prospective incumbent as yourself.

"Now I know it sounds ungrateful to say I am in any trouble. I have the very best husband who is to be found in this hemisphere—or any other hemisphere, or sphere either for the matter of that. He is making a small fortune by his pen, and I am earning what would have once seemed to me a fabulous amount by teaching. My father and mother share our suburban retreat, and are reposing, if not exactly under laurels, at least in a not undignified, and certainly not undeserved ease; and yet I have troubles to unburthen to you. I must, Mr. Briggs, constitute you my Father Confessor on the spot. Be kind enough to receive what I say to you, for the present at all events, under the seal of confession.

"Alec's last letters to you, which were really as much mine as his, will have apprised you of our position in reference to what has been correctly enough called the Ritualistic Scare. There has been, and is, a religious panic abroad, quite as bad as any of those which from time to time affect the money market, and the connexion of which with political events I never could at all understand. Our present crisis I unfortunately comprehend but too well, and wish I could forecast the issue. Perhaps I cannot better enable you to realize what I mean than by reporting to you a conversation I recently had with Alec on the subject. If this letter should expand into a series of two or three you will, I know, pardon my prolixity, because I feel we are standing at another of those crises of life, not altogether unequal to the one through which we have recently passed, and over the waves of trouble in which you, my good friend, so happily helped to tide us.

"Noticing that Alec was a good deal more away from home than usual of late, and also that he was looking worn and haggard, I asked him the reason. It was as though I had suddenly opened the safety valve of a steam engine—whatever that may be, I am sure I do not know. I expected a monosyllable, and got an oration for an answer.

"'I am so thoroughly glad you asked me that question, Elsie dear,' he said, 'because it affords me an opportunity of making an explanation which I feel is due to you.'

" ' You scarcely needed an introduction on my part, husband, to enable you to open up any subject which was interesting or troubling you, I hope. Which is it?'

" ' A little of both, Elsie.'

" ' Then pardon my saying that, in both cases—but especially as far as your trouble is concerned—I think I, as your wife, ought to have been taken into confidence. What is a wife for if not that troubles—and interests too, I have been led to hope—should be common to herself and her husband?'

" ' You are kind to say so, but I didn't want to bother you unnecessarily.'

" ' Just what the old folks said when the Zoar difficulties occurred. They expatriated me to Sam's until the tyranny was overpast, at least until they miscalculated that it would be overpast. Why they did it and you do it I cannot think. Surely it is better for me to know all gradually than to be let down flop to the bottom of the abyss; or am I such a poor nervous hysterical kind of young lady that you fear I shall "go off" or do some other conventional thing? Would you like to send me to Gower Street again? They would be so glad to see me now.'

" ' Don't jeer. Really when I come to think of it, Gower Street would be the best place for you—the only place where I could guarantee your being safe from the dangers that now seem closing in upon you.'

" ' Shall I tell you what those dangers are ?'

" ' I thought you wanted me to tell you.'

" ' But just to prove that your precautions were unnecessary, and that I guessed or otherwise knew what you are now going to tell me so mysteriously.'

" ' Tell me.'

" ' Shall I summarize the difficulties and dangers in one significant monosyllable ?'

" ' Do.'

" ' *Rome.*'

" ' How do you do it, Elsie ?'

" ' Do what ?'

" 'Look inside one. Now I have never breathed a word of this to you, and yet you read me like a book.'

" 'Yes, you have breathed a word about it, you great silly fellow, or you have been doing lately what is more emphatic still, you have been holding your tongue about it. Up to a certain point you talked and wrote of nothing but the Ritualistic Scare and the alleged Intrigue with Rome. All of a sudden you stop dead. You never mention the matter; your leaders are on the condition of the mangel wurzel crop, or the state of our merchant shipping, or some other subject equally unknown and un-interesting to you; but do you suppose I did not know you were thinking about, perhaps acting in reference to, the other and more engrossing subject all the time?'

" 'Did you?'

" 'Then again, there has been a spy in the camp.'

" 'Who is that?'

" 'Little Amy; I wonder why we never

mention that child without dwelling on her smallness. Yes, Amy has quite un- intentionally divulged something, but not all of that which is troubling you. I have forborne to pump her, because I really thought you wished me to be kept in the dark, and was content to wait for the time when I should be honoured by being taken into confidence; but, bless you, the lace- bordered pictures of St. Theresa and the Virgin, which cropped up in the prayer books, not to mention the substitution of Roman for Anglican Manuals of Devotion, told me which way the wind was blowing.'

" ' Yes, of course, you have known that for a long time; but you don't know to what purpose or with what sweeping effect that wind has blown.'

" ' That I am to learn now—at last ;' and I posed myself to listen.

" Then came the oration.

" ' I used to think,' said Alec, ' when people told me of Roman propagandism, that they were drawing upon what, to put

it mildly, was a peculiarly lively imagination. When Mrs. Grundy said that
converts to Rome (I scarcely know whether
I ought to say converts or perverts just at
present, so let us stick to the old slang and
say 'verts) that they sometimes remained
ostensibly in Anglicanism after being received into Rome, and that they did this
for purposes of proselytism, then I used to
tell that exceedingly respectable female that
she lied in her throat.'

" ' Which was decidedly not respectful on
your part.'

" ' It was not meant to be. But, Elsie,
would you be surprised to hear—as the
Attorney General said in the Tichborne
case—that Mrs. Grundy is right?'

" ' Not at all.'

" ' Ain't you scandalized at the discovery ?'

" ' Not in the least.'

" ' Indeed ! why not?'

" ' Why, because, if Mrs. Grundy had a
single atom of logic as an element in her

composition, she would see that a 'vert was bound by his or her very 'version to do all he or she could to 'vert others.'

" ' I'm uncommonly glad to hear you say so.'

" ' Why ?'

" ' Because it will prevent those who have taken such a course from appearing before you in a peculiarly odious light.'

" ' You ought to know me better, Alec ; the memory of the old philosophic days, as we called them, ought to be fresher with you than that you should suspect me of being scandalized by the circumstance of a sincere person adopting one form of faith in preference to another, or doing all they could to spread that faith which, in the glow of its very novelty, seemed to them to exhaust all truth. The interesting converts are Mrs. Fane and Amy, are they not ?'

" ' Yes. They are so anxious for you to know.'

" ' Why did they not let me know at every step whither their convictions were carrying them? They might have borne me beyond the Rubicon with them.'

" ' Do you think so?' Alec eagerly asked.

" ' I don't think so, but it might have been.'

" He tried to adopt my method and read me like a book then ; but I think I made myself utterly illegible. A woman can when she likes, Mr. Briggs, as you will one day learn.

" ' Yes, Mrs. Fane and Amy have been received into the Catholic Church.'

" ' Meaning the Roman Catholic——'

" ' Into the Roman Church. It seems to me a contradiction of terms to put any particularizing epithet before the word Catholic. When Mrs. Fane, having gone as far as Pugin could take her, parted company with him, she apprised him in the most friendly way of the fact, and, on resigning his spiritual directorship, he distinctly advised the step she has taken.'

" ' Father Pugin did this ?'

" ' Yes ; and it now seems to me, though

I was at first staggered like yourself, that there was no other course open to him. He had laboured conscientiously to prevent the issue; he went again over every argument he could muster to induce her to change her mind; but having done this, he could do no more than lay down his office and consign her to another. He told her he thought she was wrong, and warned her that she might think so when too late, but if Rome and truth seemed to her synonymous, then he could not counsel hesitation, for he should be asking her to violate conscience; so he simply gave her the address of a certain Roman Catholic priest, whom we will know only as Father Blank, if you please, but whose name and address Father Pugin had so thoroughly at his fingers' ends that one cannot help thinking Mrs. Fane's was not the first instance where he had found it necessary to make a transfer of the kind.'

" ' I daresay not.'

" ' But, Elsie, will you allow me to say

parenthetically, I am considerably disappointed that you do not lift up your hands and call this very dreadful? All my mystery has been thrown away, all the delicate device of letting the portentous secret ooze out gradually by means of picture cards and Roman manuals left about in apparent carelessness has been wasted.'

" 'Utterly.'

" 'How very disheartening! Well, perhaps I shall shock you when I tell you that I went with Mrs. Fane to Father Blank—that I listened silently to all the arguments which he most unnecessarily put forward to controvert those of Father Pugin, and prove to her that what she had done was for the salvation of her soul and her own peace of mind. I was even sent to fetch Amy; and afterwards was present when they were formally received into the Roman Communion. This must shock you.'

" 'I think it would have been more decorous if your wife had been with you.'

" ' But you really don't think it was a damnable thing to do, to kneel there and formally take one's place in the Catholic Church, and then come back as if nothing had happened and resume a position in the Anglican Communion for purposes of propagandism ?'

" ' I have told you I think it is the only proper and logical course for a 'vert. When once you are convinced that you are part and parcel of an infallible Church, and that out of the pale of that Church there is no salvation, you are bound to believe, too, that the end justifies any means for snatching brands from the burning, and folding stray sheep in that Church.'

" ' Exactly the very words Father Blank uses. Pardon me, Elsie,' said Alec, quite seriously, ' but have you been doing a little conversion on your own account ?'

" ' No, I have not ; but if I had known one thing, I would.'

" ' What's that ?'

" ' *You have, Alec;* and it was unkind not

16—2

to tell me beforehand, and give me the chance of going hand in hand with you.'

" I think one of the cruellest things a woman can do is to exercise the power we know we possess, Mr. Briggs, of making the male sex *blush*. A great big fellow such as Alec never looks so utterly helpless and foolish as when he blushes like a girl, especially in presence of one who knows him familiarly. I would almost rather see a man cry.

" Alec blushed to the very roots of his beard and moustache, and up among his prolific Antinous-curls, when I read his stupid secret; and, although I really was sorry for him, I was annoyed on my own account, and returned to the fray.

" ' Yes; if I had been deemed worthy your confidence, Alec, I might have gone with you; or if I had suspected what you were doing, if you had not fooled and deceived me quite so successfully, I might, as I said, have done a little counter-plotting on my own account, and gone over too, if only for the pleasure of greeting you on the other side, and witnessing your dismay at finding you had not left your wife behind, as you evidently wished—and still wish— to do.'

"'Elsie, dear Elsie,' the great silly fellow said, 'pray pardon me. I had no more idea of what I was doing than that child Amy had. I was carried away by Father Blank's arguments—all tending, I grant you, in the direction of my own ideas; but when I entered the sacristy of that church I had no more idea that I should emerge thence a Catholic than you had.'

"'And then when you had taken the step, you did not know how to tell me?'

"'That's just it; and that was why I was so pleased at your giving me the opportunity of telling you. Now you will take the same step too, won't you?'

"'Most certainly *not.*'

"'Not, Elsie! Shall there be division between us?'

" ' Who made the division ?'

" ' I, with my silly impetuosity, and sillier reticence.'

" ' Then as you have chosen to act singly, allow me to do the same.'

" ' And what will you do ?'

" ' Without in the least realizing any obligation to tell you, I will so far heap coals of fire on your head as not to make a mystery about it. I am going to be a 'vert too.'

" ' That's right.'

" ' But not to your opinions; no, I shall join the Particular Baptists, and then tell my pa how you have behaved to me.'

" Here Alec burst into a loud, hilarious laugh, which was particularly annoying to me, because I did not know at which portion of my threat he was making merry; whether it was at the remarkable communion for which I declared my proclivity, or at my mention of a parental appeal.'

" ' Don't guffaw,' I said, ' I hate it.'

" This made him laugh all the more. It

was a quiet chuckle now, which betokened yet more subtle mirth.

" 'You won't tell your father, Elsie, will you?'

" 'Yes, I will; because I don't think you have acted nicely, Alec, and he ought to know.'

" 'Don't tell him, please.'

" 'I will. Don't you be idiotic, and grin. Why shouldn't I tell him?'

" 'Because he's gone over, too,' he replied.

" 'What!'

" 'Your father, directly Mrs. Fane told him what had occurred, and without waiting for her to exercise her powers of propagandism, toddled off to Father Blank, and was received on his own account. Hither he comes, opportunely. He has been down to Father Pugin, to restore our habits as Brethren of the Third Order, and make our apologies at having so speedily vacated them. Well, father, I've broken it to Elsie, and she seems to bear it very well.'

"'She does nothing of the kind,' I replied. 'I am exceedingly disgusted at being left out in the cold in this way. Have *you* taken *your* wife, may I ask?'

"'No,' said my father. 'I durstn't tell Charlotte until I had secured you——'

"'Don't reckon on me, father; I'm disgusted at this duplicity. My mother and myself, like two injured individuals as we are, will go over to the Strict Baptists at once. Oh, I know what I wish.'

"'What?'

"'That I could only find Mr. Moddle—dear, injured, rejected Moddle! I would throw myself in his arms, twine mine around his bull-neck and say, "Moddle, my own Moddle, come over with me to the Particulars." He would drop down heavily on you, my venerable parent, if he knew what you had been doing.'

"Moddle was a good card to play. The mention of him made Alec jealous and frightened my father.

"Such, then, dear Mr. Briggs, is the first

instalment of my troubles with which I feel
it necessary to trouble you in your new
capacity of involuntary Father Confessor.
I am worried, because what has occurred
seems to re-introduce division between
myself and my husband. Once, and not so
long ago either, I represented belief and he
scepticism. Now the poles are reversed.
He has chosen to develop Faith solely; and
I am conscious that in his eyes I must
embody Doubt. Alec would not use the
smaller word heresy in reference to me;
but the two words stand for the same thing
in reference to his present position. I
really feel half inclined to do as my father
has done, go off to the priest on my own account, and when I come back say to Alec—

" 'There, I have done the deed. We are
once again united.'

" What shall I do ?

"On reading over again what I have
written above, I can quite fancy you saying,
' Bless the woman ! she talks of going over
to the Catholic faith and communion just as

she would of changing her gown.' I own
it reads so; but, as perhaps you will understand from our previous philosophizings,
mere forms of belief, and, still more, resultant
forms of practice, appear utterly irrelevant to
one who has known what it is to doubt the
great essentials. Get over that, as, thank
God, my husband and myself have done,
and there are really no limits to the possible
development of one's creed. Was not that
the meaning of the assertion that all things
were possible to him who believed? The
Catholic Church does embody in a very
fascinating form this development of Faith
pushed to its very ultimatum. I am not
sure that any other form of faith would
have 'fixed' my husband. Ritualism was
obviously incapable of doing so, because, as
he said, he never could get over the ille-
gality of it. He broke his shins—as he
said—over the Public Worship Act at
every step he made; and that bothered
him. He felt dishonest, without meaning
to be so, just as, directly he leavened his

belief with the smallest infusion of Private Judgment, that seemed to necessitate logically a return to his old attitude of unbelief. Where, he asked, was one to stop, if once one began to question?

" It will strike you then, perhaps, that I have nothing, or not so much, to grumble about; and really the mere writing down of my troubles seems to have relieved me wonderfully. That, I have no doubt, is, to a great extent, the rationale of auricular confession. It depends as much on the relief the penitent feels in unbosoming, as on the actual advice he gets from his director. Nay, is not the same, in a measure, the explanation of what is called the subjective influence of prayer? It lifts those who pray to a higher plane where they come in contact with a new set of laws, and so derive benefit even where the special petitions they offer up remain palpably unanswered.

" I feel just as if I were back at my old

interleaved diary again, long since cremated, except in so far as the pages which have been rescued, to form materials for our apparently inevitable story. I rather plume myself too on corresponding with a Father Confessor of my own sub rosâ. Alec has had his secret; now I have got mine. It need not be a secret long. I shall make him take a holiday, and run down to Zoar, ostensibly to look after the lawyers, but really to have a talk with you. Then you can show him these sheets. He will see there is nothing very treasonable in them; but still I can keep my secret as well as he. I have just had a little explanation with Mrs. Fane on this topic too. I thought it better to assume the tone of an injured individual at first, so this is how I commenced—

"'I scarcely think it was kind of you, my dear Mrs. Fane, to take the serious step Alec tells me you have taken, or at all events, to induce him to take the step with you without consulting me.'

"In reply, she struck an attitude, much to Amy's amusement, and forthwith became Shakspearian :—

    "' Saucy and overbold! How did you dare
        To trade and traffic with Macbeth
        In riddles and affairs of death;
        And I, the mistress of your charms,
        The close contriver of all harms,
        Was never called to bear my part,
        Or show the glory of our art?'

"'Don't be angry, Hecate,' she added, with a smile there was no resisting.

"I pouted however, and said nothing.

"'I really wish I could take the credit, or even give Father Blank the credit, of having induced your liege lord to make the very praiseworthy step in advance of his previous unbelief.'

"'He was not an unbeliever when he made it.'

"'But,' she went on, not heeding my pert parenthesis, 'he took us all by surprise, and made that step spontaneously on his own account. He quite took all our breaths away, didn't he, Amy? He commenced an

active propagandism forthwith, and hauled
in his Irvingite father-in-law in the net of
the Church.   He acted in the very spirit, if
not according to the actual letter, of the
apostolic injunction, for when converted, he
strengthened his father, instead of his
brethren.'

"'What I want to know is, why he didn't
strengthen me?—why everybody seems to
have left me out of their consideration?'

"'I didn't, for one.'

"'Surely, yes.'

"'Surely, no.'

"'Pray, how did you consider me?'

"'By keeping you carefully in the dark.
You have just that element of conservatism
in you, derived, I doubt not, from your
most exemplary mother, which would have
made you talk some of us—not me, but
Alec and Amy very likely—back into Protestantism in less than no time.   So I
thought it was better we should all make the
plunge first, and then let you exercise your
ingenuity in talking us back again.   Try.'

" ' I shall do nothing of the kind.'

" ' You will with Alec.'

" ' I certainly shall not.'

" ' I trust you not to interfere with Amy's convictions.'

" ' You may trust me just as confidently with my husband as with my pupil. I have too great a respect for honest conviction to endeavour to shake it in anybody, least of all in him.'

" ' And I am sure you must see, dear Elsie,' said the wheedling little woman, commencing her campaign on me, preparatory, I have no doubt, to an onslaught upon my 'exemplary mother,' 'how the Catholic system is exactly calculated to answer the needs of a cultured mind like Alec's, weary of the speculations of philosophy, and scared off from religion by a cold, ungenial Evangelicalism.'

" I did see this to a very great degree, but I was not going to tell her so, at least not just yet.

" ' And if suitable for him, suitable for

you too, Elsie; for you are wonderfully alike—too much alike for man and wife I sometimes think.'

" I know Mrs. Fane looks upon this as the most delicate way of flattering me; and, as a fact, I do like it, for I am very proud of Alec, as I daresay you have found out.

" And now I have news for you, definite information apart from these mere worries, which, I daresay, strike you as uneventful, though I hope not uninteresting, enough. Alec is coming to you at once : going to take you en route to our Welsh estates— or, in other words, our Castles in Spain— for I don't believe in their existence, or rather in any title of ours to them. I suppose they exist for somebody, since there is no doubt Susanna Dash was a rich woman, far richer than the mere proprietorship of Topaz would have made her. Well, Alec is coming to you, and then going to Wales, to look after these possessions of ours. He says, too, that he is overworked, and wants rest, I don't believe it. I think he has

been taking it remarkably easy of late ; and
I know exactly what his plan is. He
means to leave me for Mrs. Fane to
manipulate. Not a bad scheme ; but supposing I take the game out of their hands,
and act on my own ideas. I think I will
ask you, dear Mr. Briggs, to aid me in
being a little mysterious. Show Alec all
the letters up to the date of this, if you
like ; then let there be a dead silence ; it
will add greatly to the effect. I will write
to Alec on general topics, and have my
letters to you addressed by some one else.
Is not that quite romantic? In editing
the effusions, you can take what you like
from the esoteric and exoteric respectively,
so as to keep up the thread of the narrative.

" Aunt Patty appeared on the tapis as
soon as Alec's back was turned. Of course
all his movements are known when they
turn in the direction of Zoar ; and Sam
must be neglecting his business frightfully
by his continual absence on these so-called

Evangelizing expeditions. When Aunt Patty looked me up in our little re- treat, which, by the way, I could not help considering a huge piece of imperti- nence after all that had occurred, I allowed myself just so large a modicum of revenge as to say—

" 'So you've really found me out here, and come alone too. Hasn't Uncle Sam returned from the North of Ireland yet?'

" She thought it best to shirk the ques- tion, which she did with an unctuous smile; so I proceeded—

" 'He must have had time to convert every Catholic in Ulster; and I suppose he has sent you here on a mission to save me as a brand from the burning?'

" 'Surely you have not gone over too, Elsie?' she said, I almost believe with real anxiety.

" 'No, but I am going—going, as the auctioneers say. Would you like to wit- ness the knock-down, and see me received?'

" 'God forbid!'

" ' Well, I daresay He will, for I don't much think I shall go.'

" ' I'm delighted to hear it.'

" ' You see we are first going to take possession of our Welsh estates—Alec is down there now—and a Roman Catholic squire and squiress would be awkward, wouldn't they ?'

" I thought I might as well romance a little, as she had done in that North of Ireland business. I knew it would all be reported to Sam at Zoar, so on I went—

" ' Then, again, our settlement at Topaz Farm is only a question of time. There is a good deal of delay about these law matters, but Alec is bound to oust Uncle Edward.'

" ' Yes ?' Who does not know the latent meaning of the interrogative yes ?

" ' Yes. He will simply produce Susanna Dash's will, and the title is destroyed as far as Uncle Edward is concerned.'

" ' Yes ?'

" 'Of course I don't want you to commit yourself in our interest, because Uncle Sam is virtually involved in this, as well as Uncle Edward.'

" 'Yes?'

" 'Don't keep on saying yes, aunt, in that way; but tell me why you have honoured me with your company to-day. You haven't taken any notice of us since our marriage. Why have you become civil all of a sudden?'

" 'Your uncle does not know a word about my coming,' she said, in a tone which convinced me he did, and had sent her, 'but it seems so dreadful to let one's own flesh and blood drift to destruction for want of a word that I've——' and she began to ferret in the reticule which she always carried with her, and the contents of which were familiar enough to me.

" 'Don't give me a tract, aunt, because if you do I shall tear it up and make spills of it. Yes, it's a dreadful thing to say, I know,' for she was trying to look horrified, 'but I have grown out of Canon Ryle and Mr. Maguire——'

"'Grown up to Cardinal Manning and Monsignor Capel!'

"'Well, not quite, but next door to them. At all events I infinitely prefer them to the Evangelicals.'

"'Poor girl!'

"'Thanks for your pity. But do you really consider every Roman Catholic out of the pale of salvation?'

"'Elsie, how can you ask such a question? Of course I do.'

"'What a comfortable creed it must be.'

"'Comfortable or not, it's true.'

"'Of course, because it's your doxy. Everybody's own doxy is orthodoxy. Do you know, auntie, what is the chief thing that inclines me to become a Catholic?'

"'Meaning a Papist. No; what?'

"'Your unsparing abuse of them. There must be something good in the creed or community that it is worth while to be always attacking. There is an old proverb to the effect that it is only at fruit trees thieves throw stones.'

"'I see you are hopelessly gone. I may as well go too,' said Aunt Patty, rising, and shouldering her umbrella and reticule.

"'What, to Rome?' I answered, pretending to misunderstand her. 'Do. Let's make a family party. I will if you will.'

"'Not to Rome, but Gower Street,' she said, with a scowl.

"'Oh, that's quite another pair of sleeves, as the French say,' I replied.

"'Thank God it is.'

"'Amen. How go on T. and P.?'

"'Will you come and see?'

"'What! and be prayed at as a scarlet lady in embryo? Not if I know it. No; I suppose I must follow my husband's lead, unless—shall we try it?—unless we can get him back.'

"'Oh do,' said the poor deluded creature, rummaging at the very foundations of her reticule again. 'Won't you give him a tract?'

" 'If you want to keep him fixed where he is, yes. The very sight of one of your Protestant broadsides would make him shut his eyes to every argument in favour of Anglicanism.'

" ' But you think there are hopes of your husband ?'

" ' If Protestants only won't badger him, yes.'

" ' And your poor father——'

" ' Poor in the sense that his affectionate brothers and sisters have plucked him bare to the very bone; but if you mean as regards his conversion——'

" ' Perversion !'

" ' Well, any 'version you like ; he simply describes himself as being jolly as a sand-boy. To be a member of an infallible Church, he says, saves one such a deal of trouble in making up one's mind.'

" ' How like him !'

" ' Yes, it's characteristic; and I think in that respect Catholicism suits him. I shouldn't wonder if he remained where he is!'

" 'And Mrs. Fane, your—your——'

" 'My mistress—say it if you like. My very dear kind friend, as I call her, has found in Rome rest and peace which I am convinced she could have found nowhere else. You can't stretch us all on a bed of Procrustes, aunt.'

" 'I don't know who Procrustes was, some of your mediæval saints, I suppose, but you *can* stretch everybody on the bed of Protestantism.'

" 'There would be some very strange bedfellows if you did. To a cultured mind fond of taking things on trust, and bored by having to think for itself, the Roman is the very system of all others. For her it was the sole alternative to utter worldliness.'

" 'It *is* worldliness,' snapped my aunt.

" 'Now you are uncharitable, and I shall change the subject. Have you heard anything about my old lover, Mr. Moddle?'

" 'Yes,' replied my aunt, trying to look very mysterious, but, I could see, burning to tell a fib. 'Yes, I have seen and heard a good deal of Mr. Moddle lately. He is in excellent hands.'

" ' A lady's ?'

" ' No.'

" ' Then Mr. Morphine's.'

" ' Ask me no questions, Elsie.'

" ' And then you will tell me no lies.'

" ' I never lie.'

" ' Not about the North of Ireland ?'

" I wanted her to go, so fired off this shot, which I knew would tell. She was off in an instant, having extracted a half promise from me to go and see her at Gower Street. I would undergo even T. and P. if I could see that old turncoat Moddle in course of conversion. I wonder what his move can be now. Have the Irvingites discarded him ?

" To take stock for one moment of my interesting batch of 'verts, they seem to me, dear Mr. Briggs, to represent every phase of religious thought. Glancing outside the charmed pale, Aunt Patty is one of the snarling Controversialists who, as Tom

Hood says, 'think they're pious when they're only bilious.' Her Protestantism is of that acrid cantankerous kind which I verily believe is a far more potent agent for sending folks Romeward than all the Ritualistic propagandism in the world, if such exists. I say 'if,' even now, when I have been a bit behind the scenes. I don't really believe Father Pugin is playing into the hands of Father Blank; though when the former sees that the plunge must be made, he accepts the inevitable very calmly. But it is this low-minded odium theologicum of ecclesiastical Aunt Patties—and their name is legion—which renders the plunge necessary. It's bad form, as the slang goes; and when you have said that you have gone a long way towards accounting for the secession of a man like my husband—the first on my list of 'verts. As to my father, it is, as I have said, that a mere spiritual indolence has taken him to, and I believe will keep in, Rome. I doubt whether one ought to seek his return; for in a system where private judgment had any scope at all, he would be the prey of the first unprincipled Mr. Moddle who crossed his orbit. In his present position he is armed with triple brass. Requiescat. I wonder my mother has not followed him. It matters little to what religious body men or women like her outwardly belong. They are the very salt of the system they choose; or rather, they have a soul so infinitely above all systems that they seem already to have realized the perfect unanimity of a sphere beyond the present, where all— no matter from what school or system they come — shall join in singing the song of the redeemed which they alone can sing.

" Would not that make a fine peroration for a sermon, Mr. Briggs? You are welcome to it, if you would fain rouse your torpid prospective parishioners at East Zoar. I think if I knew any sect where women took orders, I would join that; for I think I could preach. The only sects I know are the Shakers and the Quakers, and either one or the other of those names is sufficient to scare me off from the body that owns it. How much our religious profession is a matter of taste after all!

"At present, then, I am out in the cold; and *for* the present shall, I think, remain so. There is something rather fascinating in this kind of religious Bohemianism. I remember reading of some one's conversion to Romanism—I think it was Cardinal Manning's own—and being particularly struck with the way in which he described the negative phase which intervened between his secession from the old and his adoption of the new faith. I mean, of course, old and new in reference to himself, just as I write 'conversion' instead of 'perversion.' If there is one thing I thank Providence for it is that I am, I believe, free from the littlenesses of religionism. One expects such littlenesses, because religion is human and shadowed with the imperfections of humanity; but it is a great

thing to feel conscious of being above them ;
to feel, not what I used to call a philosophic
scorn of all religions, but what I believe to
be a true Christian toleration of and, to a
certain extent, sympathy with all. I
honestly declare I can go into a gorgeous
Catholic cathedral and bend in adoration
before the elevated Host, and then go across
the road to a simple Protestant parish
church, where the State parson is preaching
(as I know he practises) moral virtue, and
feel just as much at one with him, or with
his Nonconformist neighbour in the white-
washed chapel round the corner of the next
by-street. Sectaries call this Indifferentism,
and say I am of no use to any community. I
am weary of communities and organizations
of all kinds. Even if I do follow Alec's
lead and gravitate to Rome, I feel I shall
do that as an act based on my own private
judgment, and retain my religious in-
dividuality quite independently of Church,
confessor, or what not. Is not that an
argument for going? It would be delicious

for Alec and myself to be at one again outwardly as we are inwardly.

"I wonder if I weary you with these details, Mr. Briggs. Psychologically I think such problems are not without their interest; but parsonically they should possess an import far deeper. You will, no doubt, have to deal with cases of conscience when you become pastor of St. Simon Magus; though East Zoar used not to be very sensitive in my days.

"There is still one of my batch of 'verts of whom I have said little—my dear pupil Amy. She has not yet been of sufficient importance to claim many words; but the change seems to have, if I may so say, converted her physically from a child to a woman, as well as from an Anglican to a Roman Catholic. There is something very true to nature in the way the Romish Church takes up and consecrates childhood to the service of the sanctuary. Without making the child precocious or unduly conscious of its own importance, Rome does manage to impress its plastic nature with a sense of responsibility, and, above all, to make the child love church and take an interest in its services. I felt this in a modified form with the Cathedral service at Zoar ; but I never saw it realized so thoroughly as in the transition of dear Amy from mere insipid young-ladyism to all the ardour of a dévouée.

" ' Dear Elsie,' she said one evening, when I had been arraying her for taking part in a procession at Benediction, ' I should be so perfectly happy in my new faith if only you belonged to it too—if I could only walk hand in hand with you in to-night's procession. Do you never think of taking the step we seem all to have taken except yourself ?'

" ' I have a majority against me certainly, Amy,' I replied, 'and it would be idle to deny, dearest, that your examples affect me very deeply, and make me inclined to follow you ; but——'

" ' But what ?'

" 'I must be thoroughly convinced before I change.'

" 'It seems presumptuous for me to talk to you, Elsie, who are so much older and more clever than myself, but I don't believe any of us were convinced when we made the step. For myself I only followed my dear mother, and conviction came afterwards.'

" 'Amy,' I rejoined, pretending to look very serious, 'do you know you have unintentionally offended me?'

" 'Oh, Elsie, what have I done?'

" 'You have done nothing; but you have said something which offends me mortally.'

" 'Yet you own it was unintentional. What have I said?'

" 'You called me clever. If you value my friendship, never do that again.'

" 'I will not if you do not like it. But you *are* clever, you know, Elsie.'

" 'I am not clever, and I won't be called so. It's an old grievance of mine. People always would call me clever, and I believe that when they do so, they mean to say I am only clever and nothing else—all head and no heart. I always take that word clever to be synonymous with unwomanly. You don't mean it so, dearest, I am quite aware, but that is the idea it conveys to me.'

" ' Then I will never call you clever again, though I must still apologize to you for trying to influence you in favour of the beautiful faith of our adoption. How perfectly happy we should all be—Mr. Lund and mamma, as well as my humble self—if we could only feel you were at one with us.'

" ' Would you ?'

" ' Oh yes, Elsie. Do you know I have an idea ?'

" ' Nonsense ! One whole idea ! Have I succeeded in imparting so much ? What is it ?'

" ' You will laugh, I know, but still I will tell you. It is this—you have taught me a very large portion of what I know in secular matters———'

" ' One whole idea !'

" ' Lots of great and noble ideas, dear Elsie. You have made me love the learning I once hated, and given an interest to subjects which other teachers succeeded in making dry as dust.'

" ' Well ?'

" ' Well, now, I feel I should like to repay you in the only way I ever can repay you, by giving you my own simple faith, which is making me so happy, and I am sure would make you so too. Will you let me, child as I am, lead you, the grown woman, the——'

" ' Don't say " clever," Amy.'

" ' Well, I won't, though it's hard to find another word that expresses what I want to say. Let me lead you by the hand to dear Father Blank, and say, " Here is Elsie, come to be received into the Church. She does not quite see her way clearly yet ; but she will, as I did. Take her from me." Will you do this ?'

" I never was so near ' going ' in my life,

Mr. Briggs. I thought of that millennial expression, 'A little child shall lead them.' Why not let the sweet child lead me as she proposed? Later on, when I was quiet at home, I thought of instances which had come to my knowledge where tiny children had won strong men or worldly women to God—thought of little crosses standing over graves in the Zoar churchyard, where I knew that little innocents had literally glorified God in their deaths, by turning the hearts of their bereaved parents heaven-wards; and really that was the guise that little Amy seemed to wear. She seemed to have passed, by death to the old faith, on to new life, and now to be stretching out the shining hand from some purer sphere to me still lingering down among the mists and darkness of the valley. I felt half disposed to take a sheet of Alec's ecclesiastical note-paper and write, 'Dear Amy, I yield. You *shall* take me by the hand, and lead me whither you will.' Since Alec has joined the Roman communion he always writes on paper with a Latin cross embossed in silver upon it. He says he needs some such reminder that whatever he does should be done in the name of his Master. For the same reason he wears a silver cross on his watch-chain. The reason he gave was a striking one. The import of the cross itself, he said, I needed not that he should tell me; but why he used a silver one in both instances was because in the Temple of old the golden decorations signified Divine Glory, the silver, *Human Purity.* ' I want above all things to be pure, dear wife,' he said.

"I gazed at the silver cross as I sat, hesitating whether I should write to Amy, and the words of the Paradise-hymn kept ringing through my mind all that evening; but I did not write the letter. The fit passed over; and when Amy came smiling to me the next morning, and said, ' Well, Elsie, have you slept upon it? Shall I lead you by the hand?' I replied, far more grumpily I fear than I ought—

" ' No, Amy, let us go to our work. I'm not convertible just yet.'

" Child that she was, she could not look below the surface, or she would have seen that a word would have done the work then. She did not see it—did not speak. Her bright eyes filled with tears of disappointment as, with her accustomed docility, she followed me in a learned dissertation on the literature of the Tudor period."

CHAPTER VII.

ELSIE'S POSTSCRIPT.

EAREST ALEC,—How ridiculous one feels writing to one's husband! Every tender expression — even that conventional superlative with which I garnish your name—seems to belong to a previous state of existence. I don't mean that married people care for one another less, or love one another less (you always said I was shirking the truth when I used the former term in our old heterodox days of flirtation); but they show it less. When the inward spiritual grace is there, what need of the outward visible sign? But I forgot, I must not talk theology to you now. Anyhow, all the people I know—notably Sam and Patty—who fondle one another ad nauseam in public, fight like cats in private. Take comfort, then, that I am not demonstrative, and that I pen our connubial love letters almost under protest.

"So you can find out nothing about the Welsh estates (let me recommend you to 'try Spain'), and legal matters at Zoar are in statu quo. That is a way things have in Zoar; but here I should recommend you to 'try London.' Do as you propose, get a good active town lawyer, and have the Topaz business settled one way or the other. To judge by the fact of Percy being still at large, the metropolitan authorities do not seem to be much more active or intelligent than the West country ones; still I would not leave a stone unturned.

"I have been trying—or rather I ought in justice to say *we* have been trying—our little powers in furtherance of this object; you will be surprised to hear in what direction, and with what success. If I had you here, I should take you by your broad shoulders, stare into your big brown eyes, with mine, which you are rude enough to

call unripe gooseberries, and make you
guess who had called to see me. It would
take a long time to do that by letter, so
I will tell you at once—

" Moddle !

" He came just as I was going to Amy ;
and do you know my occult power of reading people through and through, informed
me that he had not come to see me. Just
a flash of suspicion crossed my mind for the
moment that he had come to make love to
me in your absence. You would say that is
the idea that always does occur first to a
woman; but no, I saw that was not what
he wanted. I had my bonnet on, and told
him I was going to my pupil.

" ' I know,' he said ; ' Miss Fane.'

" ' Yes.'

" ' Take me with you.'

" ' Do you want some elementary instruc-
tion, and a pretty fellow-pupil ?' I inquired.

" ' No,' he replied ; ' I want to be introduced to Mrs. Fane.'

" ' What in the name of goodness for ?'

" ' Do you mind my making a little secret of that ?'

" ' Not in the least.' And the horrid Bluebeard kind of leer on his face, which I remembered so well on a certain memorable occasion, told me what he did want.

" ' Shall I tell you,' I continued, ' why you want to be introduced to Mrs. Fane ?'

" ' If you can.'

" ' You are looking out for another wife.'

" ' How did you know that ?'

" ' That's my secret.'

" ' Well, you may say it's our secret; for since you refused me so decidedly, you know I must have felt desolate.'

" ' Never mind that; let bygones be bygones. Why should you, from all the women in both hemispheres, select this one, about whom you know nothing ?'

" ' I know more than you think; and if you don't mind my going with you, I will tell you as we go along what I know and why I wish this result.'

" Then he imparted to me his design to

marry money. He talked about blighted
affections, &c., and I told him unromantically to shut up. He would like to marry
a woman of the world with money enough
to enable him to pursue his studies, yet at
the same time to enjoy every now and then
a peep into the glittering scene from
which, by his student-life, he had exiled
himself. He talked like a kind of nineteenth century Arbaces, located in London
instead of Pompeii; and I formed a deep
scheme as we wended our way through the
streets to Mrs. Fane's abode.

"By singular good fortune, when I got
to the schoolroom, leaving Moddle in the
drawing-room, I found Mrs. Fane there
alone, and I am sorry to say I was undignified enough to burst into such a
violent fit of laughter, that, in the absence
of any apparent cause, I believe she thought
I was either hysterical or had what poor
old Aunt Rachel would have termed the
family failing upon me.

"'Are you insane?' she asked.

" ' Almost. I've brought you something.'

" ' What is it ?'

" ' Guess.'

" ' I never guessed anything in my life.
Tell me.'

" ' A lover.'

" ' A what ?'

" ' No ; a lover. Somebody come to propose for your hand.'

" ' Who ?'

" ' Moddle.'

" At the mention of that ineuphonious
name she laughed as insanely as I had
done ; and we were nearly black in the face
when Amy entered in a state of wonderment.

" ' What *is* the matter ?' she demanded.

" ' Only a new papa for you, Amy,' I
said.

" ' I shan't see the man ; he must be
mad.'

" ' He may be mad ; but you must see
him, to oblige me.'

"'And oblige you by listening to his proposal?'

"'Not only so, but by accepting him.'

"'Thank you.'

"'On two conditions.'

"'What are they?'

"'First that he 'verts. You could not marry a Protestant, of course.'

"'That I certainly could not; but secondly?'

"'That he tells you where Percy is.'

"'Does he know?'

"'I feel no doubt of it'—and here I need not say we became serious, Alec. 'Dear Mrs. Fane, you really may be the means of doing us a service through this madman. I don't mean to say he is mad for falling in love with you, of course, but mad to have the impudence to avow it.'

"'Mad all round. But tell me, do you really think I can do any good in this way?'

"'I not only think, but am sure of it. You know when an idea does come to me in this way, I trust it.'

"'You have had reason to. Well, I will

see him. You and Amy go into the back drawing-room quietly. You can hear through the folding doors, and I by no means wish my interview with my lover at first sight to be a private one.'

"We went.

"Moddle broke ground beautifully, for Mrs. Fane would not even let me introduce him. A widow is not like a blushing maid in these matters, she assured me. Moddle was really almost graceful, and quite pathetic in his apologies for this eccentric course, and his picture of the loneliness which had shadowed his recent life.

"'You know something—much, perhaps —of me from my old friend and pupil, Mrs. Lund,' he said. 'May I venture to hope that knowledge induces you to regard my suit with favour?'

"'It can scarcely be so, Mr. Moddle,' replied Mrs. Fane, acting her part consummately in looks as well as voice; for Amy and I took turns in peeping through the keyhole.

"'Why not?'

" 'Do you forget my recent conversion ?'

" 'No.'

" 'Would you risk a marriage with one of another faith ?'

" 'I would,' answered Moddle, quite brightening up at the way his suit seemed to be prospering. 'But perhaps you would not ?'

" 'Not only so, but I would not listen to a proposal, certainly would not give a reply as to the state of my affections under such circumstances. Listen, Mr. Moddle. I like the boldness of your scheme. There is a spice of knight-errantry about it which I thought had quite gone out of fashion in these degenerate days; but the man who approaches me with a proposal of marriage, must approach as a son of the Church.'

" 'There need be no difficulty about that, *dear* Mrs. Fane,' he rejoined.

" 'Stand off, sir. I cannot allow you even to touch my hand until that pre-liminary difficulty is got over; and sup-posing that surmounted, I should still exact another condition——'

"'Of accepting me?'

"'Of even giving you an answer.'

"'And that is——'

"'I will tell you. You know the whereabouts of Percy Llewellyn — the *murderer!*'

"'Humph.'

"'You hum and haw. Let me ring the bell.'

"Mr. Moddle hesitated, but it was only for a moment.

"'Let us dispose of the other difficulty first,' said the old hypocrite, evidently quite anxious to be 'verted.

"'On second thoughts, no. I reverse the order of my conditions. The whereabouts of Percy Llewellyn first; then the conversion; then my reply. Demur to these, and I will desire the servant to show you out.'

"'You are cruel.'

"'I am quite content that you should think so. I am inflexible.'

"'Evidently.'

" 'Now, not another word, but Percy Llewellyn's present address. I will certify that; you, while I am doing so, can go to Father Blank, whose direction I will give you in exchange. Come back to me a Catholic, and then we shall be in a position to treat. Mind if you say any other word, even of preface, except the actual address, I shall consider that a refusal of my preliminaries, and ring the bell.'

" She stood with the rope in her hand, and I removed my eye from the keyhole to apply my ear, as Mr. Moddle whispered an address to her.

" I could not hear it.

" 'So far, so good. I shall see that you are correct, and in the interim here is Father Blank's address. Go to him at once and come back as good a Catholic as you can in a short space of time.'

" 'You will not let Llewellyn know I gave the address?'

" 'My business just now is to impose conditions, not to accept them; but I won't be hard upon you. No; he shall not know you have peached upon him—that is the word, I believe.'

"She rang him out, and entered with such a flushed face, that she might really have been an inexperienced damsel like her own daughter fresh from her first offer.

" 'Did I not do it beautifully?'

" 'Excellently. Where is Percy?'

" 'I shall not tell you. You have put this matter in my hands; leave me to follow it up. I am off at once.'

" 'Whither?'

" 'Whither? Why, to Scotland Yard, of course. We will have no more bungling in this business. How glad I am your husband is out of the way.'

" 'Why?'

" 'I have a fancy to manage this affair myself; so go to work, and leave me to my detectives.'

"We went to our work, and Mrs. Fane returned after some hours, as taciturn and mysterious as a detective herself. She

would only tell us that Percy was *not* taken ;
no more.

"In the evening, Mr. Moddle returned
with a note from Father Blank, saying that
he had made his profession, and was
virtually a son of the Church.

"'Will that do, dear Mrs. Fane? May
I now call you so?'

"'You may now call me so. Yes, that
will do.'

"'You found the address correct?'

"'Quite.'

"'And is—Llewellyn—taken?'

"'Never mind. You *don't* mind, do
you?'

"'Not much.'

"'I thought so. Yes, you have fulfilled
your conditions to the letter, and I am now
prepared to listen respectfully to your proposal.'

"'Respectfully! Use a more tender
word, dear madam.'

"'Our acquaintance, my dear sir, has
been so brief——'

" ' But delightful.'

" ' But delightful, as you say. Then you know nothing as to my position—my means. I have a daughter—a young, un-married daughter—Mr. Moddle.'

" ' I know it all. I seek to know no more. It is for yourself I ask ; means and position are quite secondary matters with me.'

" Could he only have known that I, to whom he had confessed that position was everything, was then and there eaves-dropping !

" ' And do you really mean to say that, with the impetuosity of youth, you—a— well, a middle-aged widower—make me an offer of your hand on the spot ?'

" ' Yes.'

" ' And expect me to answer you equally offhand ?'

" ' Yes, oh yes ! why not ?'

" ' Only that it seems like going back to boys and girls again.'

" ' Be boys and girls again, dear Mrs.

Fane,' he said, sinking, Lothario-like, on his knees; 'I love you—adore you! Say, do you love me? Will you have me?'

" ' No !'

" And that was all Mr. Moddle got for his 'version, and his treason to his friend."

www.ingramcontent.com/pod-product-compliance
Lightning Source LLC
Chambersburg PA
CBHW020843020726
47497CB00005B/1240